THE

SILVER

Hearted

THE
SILVER

A NOVEL

DAVID McCONNELL

ALYSON books

The Silver Hearted

Copyright © 2009 David McConnell

Published by Alyson Books
245 West 17th Street, Suite 1200, New York, NY 10011
www.alyson.com

ALYSON*books*

Library of Congress Cataloging-in-Publication data is on file.

ISBN 978-1-59350-140-2

10 9 8 7 6 5 4 3 2 1

Cover design by Michael Fusco, *michaelfuscodesign.com*
Book interior by Neuwirth & Associates, Inc.

Printed in the United States of America
Distributed by Consortium Book Sales and Distribution
Distribution in the United Kingdom by Turnaround Publisher Services Ltd.

for friends suddenly remembered, though we've been
out of touch for years

I can offer provisional proof of this in the simple fact that the sun
has addressed me for years in human speech . . .

Daniel Paul Schreber

THE
SILVER
Hearted

1

A THOUSAND YEARS before any of this happened, I was rich
and bored and living in the famous city of Z. Something came
over me. Even before I got the bad news from the five trustees,
something changed. For several days I felt a paralyzing frustration,
sexual, occupational. I longed—the longing was so balky it wasn't
clear what exactly I was longing for. I longed for a subject in my
life. I hunted sex but came up with nothing. I cravenly abandoned
my idiosyncratic numismatic research. I stopped calling people I
knew. The fifth day was eerily overcast and warm. A friend who'd
been wondering about me stopped by. We drank a few bottles of
beer, and he innocently bored me. I hustled him out. Just before
it set, the sun dropped below the distant margin of the cloud layer
and cast a pale, swelling glow on a table of photographs in silver

and leather frames. Mom and Dad, some famous but staid ancestors, the house I'd grown up in, me as a camp counselor showing a crowd of boys a leaf of edible yarrow.

Explosively impatient, I jumped out of the chair and folded my arms at the window. Down on the street dusk accreted like the ordinary shadow it really is. The August breeze and perfumes, the glaze of a rain shower I hadn't noticed except as a strange hiss too soft to question fifteen minutes ago, even the yellowish dung of carriage horses thatching the gutters, it all had a plangent clarity in that softening light. My senses were heightened, and at the same time they distracted me from whatever it was I wanted. Not from the urgency of wanting it, though. A long way off, roiling clouds of locomotive steam vented from the great glass shed of Z's Southern Station. The sun shone through, and the station glowed like a lantern with a small ruddy flame inside.

My senses told me I was right here. I was in Z this August evening, the third, about to turn twenty-nine and in the grip of melancholy freedom. My parents were dead. I was long finished at Z's university. Tonight, if I felt like it, I could go anywhere. *Trebizond, Trebizond, Trebizond*, a lone horse clip-clopped on the street. Something seemed to be speaking in the voice of sensation. Opportunity—illusory maybe—quieted all interior babble. And all the other, the many other, illusions of my life seemed on the verge of fainting dead away, leaving me in—I don't know what state. As if I might really do something.

The trustees were in touch the following day. They hemmed and hawed. As they saw it, I'd go from rich to penniless—or all but—in a month. It's surprisingly difficult to lose so much so fast.

Exceedingly rare. Mismanagement, embezzlement had nothing to do with it. The trustees themselves were horrified. My parents had imposed rigid and eccentric rules on the money they left behind. The plan had come to ruin.

My reaction wasn't what I would have expected. I didn't know what not having money was like. I felt naked, unburdened, giddy. Even the fear was sweet. Over the next few days, I kept myself busy packing things in boxes (for no reason I could pinpoint) and drank heavily. This seemed like the natural continuation of the strange frustration I'd felt before. I was constantly changing my mind. I was going to call a friend, then didn't. I was going to go to South America, then I didn't want to. I was going to find work in a museum, then I decided that was a bad idea. I ate in expensive restaurants. I had no care for the little money I had left. I slept badly. I'd never felt so powerless. I was happy.

My little yellow dog got caught up in my excitement. He did a jig whenever I came home. At night in bed he pressed his back against my belly with almost human sighs. Cozying up like a child, he kept looking over his shoulder to see if I was still awake behind him. Instead of sleeping, I played the game of staring at him. When the dog had checked on me four or five times like this and found my eyes fixed on him each time, he snorted, leapt out of bed and did his jig on the floor in maddened delight. Then he jumped back in to nestle against me again.

I saw a few friends, but I didn't confide. Their interests and the fussy practicalities of their lives struck me as pallid. I kept finding myself awake, abuzz, at three or four in the morning. I'd go out to dives. I'd strike up conversations with strangers, playing the big man in queasy spasms, buying drinks for them. This was how I met the plump, feline, faintly amused older man who gave me a job. I had a notion he was a criminal. When the subject of work first came up, I was able to sound amazingly firm and self-convinced. I thought I'd snowed him. I didn't realize that it was just my *pretending* to deserve a job that so pleased Dadi Anton, owner of a small casino.

When I woke in the early evening of the following day, I felt better than I ever had. It was my first job. My little dog was full of attentions. I sat naked on the bed, and he licked my foot, as fully absorbed as an artist. Thinking I wanted to go to the kitchen, he loped to the kitchen door. But I went to the bathroom. He hurried to follow me. He peered over the edge of the toilet bowl to watch the burbling water ripple concentrically. He winced at stray droplets. I shook my head, smiling disbelievingly, because I had a job. I reached down and ruffled the dog's unrisen hackles. "Dog," I said. "I've been paying so little attention to you. I've been worried. Now everything's better." The dog's forebody salaamed. He sprang up and yipped playfully. The best thing about my new job was that, sometime next year, I'd get a chance to travel.

2

AT ABOUT FIVE PM on the first Monday of April of the following year I was alone in the large upper room of a hong in the city of B. I had to do the heavy lifting myself. No one could help me. Mark, Joe, Chris, Charlie, Spit, Seymour, Old Ol, Kirbie, Florindo, Kev, Legs, Mr. Haver—I'm putting their names down for a reason—these men worked in the hong in one capacity or another. I'd gotten to know them a little over the past days. They were all downstairs. The high-windowed upper room had been a ballroom when this particular hong—Bottom hong—was built as a social club for the walled foreign concession (in a more peaceable time—a long time ago). Now the room was stripped, faded, nearly empty except for my boxes. I had to move them myself.

The boxes were heavy. I could just clean-and-jerk one to my

shoulder, stagger to keep my balance and carry the thing across the worn ballroom floor. The box edge cut into my neck. Or I could use my forearms like a forklift, go dangerously swaybacked and waddle forward. The box rubbed the tendons at my biceps painfully. I could take a box by its rope handles and shamble forward stooped. That was least awkward, but it was hard on my back, and I kept barking my shins on the side of the box.

An urgent but—like all our thoughts at the time—slightly out-of-true idea occurred to me. What if I died? For we were in the middle of a battle, a siege, to be precise. The radiant confusion of the emergency made it almost impossible to have realistic thoughts apart from the ones involved in getting done what had to be done. I eased the box to the floor. I detached the loose company label from the top and wrote a few lines on the blank, glue-crusted side. Dark clouds had moved in. I could just read the lines by panning a little light from the open loading bay, which had been punched through the ballroom wall and shored with tole. The essence of my job: "Fitzable—US$2,000 Mrs. Crumb—US$9,000 Diaglott—US$2,500 Mr. Jeff Langlais—US$7,000 Mr. Tom Langlais—US$1,500 Lead Partner, Mr. Dadi Anton—US$14,000 TOTAL—US$36,000."

The afternoon storm was rising. The wind sketched one or two ostrich feathers of fine dust on the ballroom floor next to the loading bay. The noise outside, the constant shouting downstairs, maybe panic itself, made for a paradoxical interior quiet. I exercised my sore arms a moment. I walked to the bay to check on my treasure and the weather outside. The wind dried the film of my eyes, which promptly wept. The whiplashed palms of B rose and fell like flails. Overhead, a violet thunderhead writhed to impressive emotional effect, as if heaven were involved in what was going on. But this storm never came. Like a grandiose false cadence it soon dissipated, leaving behind the usual monotonous heat. I folded the company label carefully and slipped it into my pocket. I didn't need the reminder. Those names and numbers were inscribed in memory. They were the people who, in consortium, had shipped with me. The figures told how much each had put in. If I were killed and all records lost, the note might be discovered and used to divide whatever remained of the treasure of 36,000 silver dollars stored in my twenty-four blue boxes. That was my idea, punctilious yet a little off, out-of-true. What would I care, if I were dead?

I thought the claims of the shippers, not the most honest people in the world—just the opposite, in fact—might be exaggerated. I had no idea how closely allied they were. Apart from the day of the murder, I'd dealt only with Dadi Anton. I found his brutality chilling just because he kept it so well hidden. Not that anyone fell for his tallowed-seeming dismay every time voices were raised in his casino office or when I laughed at the preposterous pseudonyms of his shipping partners. Nothing about Dadi Anton was to be believed. Nevertheless his trust in me—this job—was eerily inescapable. It filled me with a kind of happiness.

If there was anything to be glad for about the insurrection (that's what they called it in-country, though the word makes things sound more organized than they were), it was that the long-anticipated fighting had broken out before I'd made any purchases. Worrying about some unwieldy cargo while the city was going up in flames would have been a lot worse than the problem I did face.

My ship, the *Clay*, had gone downriver for some small repairs. Depending on the course of the fighting and on the relationship between my shippers and the companies that controlled the concession, the *Clay* might be requisitioned by the government, or it might try to slip away from the turmoil altogether, leaving me behind. Meanwhile, the twenty-four boxes were here at Bottom hong, twelve of them still stacked against the graffittoed ballroom wall. I had to get them safely out of B.

As for investing the money somewhere else, I'd been given unusual liberty for a supercargo. I wasn't, strictly speaking, a supercargo at all, so much as an agent or independent trader. I was given this liberty because the silver was—I was pretty certain—dirty money that had to come back to Z along a clean paper trail. I could go wherever—Soledad, Annampour, Pernambuco, Trebizond. My freedom was circumscribed in one way only. If I returned with a loss on the treasure, even a negligible loss, I'd be out. And if I were thrown out, I fully believed—because I knew a bit about Dadi Anton and his business—I'd be killed, maybe beaten to death the way Clancy Rasmussen had been by the "Langlais" brothers last winter. That murder, in a restaurant supply warehouse in suburban Z, happened in the course of my sole "meeting" with my shippers.

I didn't trust anyone with the twenty-four boxes. Only when I was alone with them was I a tiny bit relaxed. The problem now was that I couldn't carry the boxes all at once. Small as they were, together they weighed nearly a ton. It was out of the question to leave any of them unguarded or even to let one out of my sight. My solution was to move them, in batches of twelve, on an open pallet I could watch.

The pallet rested on a rusting gantry platform built at the lip of the second storey ballroom's makeshift bay. I'd made a pyramid of the first twelve boxes on the pallet. I hooked an octopus of chains to the four rope slings running under the boards of the pallet. The gantry had inverted rails that ran on trestles along the side of the building. The donkey engine that powered the system throbbed when the operator threw his forked lever. The slaved chains were drawn up until the pallet levitated. After dangling from the track a moment while the engine changed pitch, the pallet—pendulous, hesitating—began to glide alongside the hong, over the one-storey godown on shore and out over the muddy river. (Locally, the companies' main storage facilities were called hongs. Godowns were smaller warehouses on the water, more convenient for loading and unloading.)

I stepped onto the gantry platform to watch it. From there I could see the engine operator, Old Ol, below me. The man had been happy enough to be asked to do his job. The favor had cost me nothing, a few dollars. It was a break from battle, for which none of us was trained or prepared. The man's nose wobbled loosely when rubbed by the greasy back of his wrist.

At the far end of the track, out over the river, the chains started to unspool, and the pallet sank onto the afterdeck of a side-wheeler riverboat—the *Myrrha*. There, I watched a shirtless, blondish boy heave the boxes from the pallet and stack them nearby, still within my sight. For this work I'd paid him lavishly,

twenty dollars, an insane amount. My idea had been to buy his
loyalty if he was going to handle my treasure. His pale face turned
up. His eyes found me on my perch of rusting ironmongery, and
he appeared to smile. I wasn't certain.

The wind was strong. I kept getting stung by debris, fragments
of browned palm leaf. Shading my eyes against them, I turned
my back on the river and looked over the city. Just seeing some
of the taller buildings beyond the fortified hongs made me kneel
instinctively. We'd learned minarets and high-rises were infested
with snipers.

Many of the buildings smoked. Some blazed. Yet in a walled
enclosure I could see an old woman sweeping her arm over
packed earth as she scattered seed for pullets. And in quite a
few windows I noticed the fickle blue light of TV sets. These
glimpses of complacency were bizarre. The country's single TV
station only broadcast reruns of expired European and American
shows, always a decade or two out of date. Expats rarely watched
TV, because the old shows gave them such an eerie sense of dis-
placement in time. That was too much added to the strangeness of
this place. They wanted to get their jobs done and get out.

Over the general roar I heard Old Ol shouting a creaky syllable
from below: "Eh? Eh?" Somehow I understood him. Through the
iron grate I was standing on he'd watched me turn toward the
city. He wanted to know how things looked. Moving to catch his
weepy eyes through the grate, I managed, "Not too bad. A couple
of fires." There were a lot of fires, but I still had twelve more
boxes to load. My shoulders were hot and sore. I backed up a
little at a gust of wind.

One of the crew, Kirbie, who played medic, had broken open a package of drugs destined for the Lutheran missionaries to the Karak Indians but undeliverable now. Last night we'd more or less humanely killed all our pets with injections of sodium pentobarbital. Their bodies formed dim mounds under a tarp at the front of the ballroom, where the high windows facing the city were sealed by steel shutters. Out of the wind I leaned against the tole jamb of the loading bay so I could keep an eye on the *Myrrha's* afterdeck. But I kept glancing back into the ballroom, not at my remaining boxes but at the dead animal hillocks.

It struck me only now that there'd been something off about the slaughter. In a flash of uncanny clarity, personal feeling—the love of my lost dog—was dredged up and urgently discarded as if by the bottom-scraping breaths my lungs kept heaving. Hauling silver had been more exercise than I was used to. That clarity, the small impression that something was amiss, felt fatal to me. A mistake had been made. But thinking about it, even awareness of it, would take me out of the action. Only doomed men thought like this in the middle of battle. Still, why had we killed the animals?

Last night's reasoning was insane. We'd killed our pets to prevent their being eaten. The "insurrectionists" were unfathomable. They reveled in savagery. In the worst case we'd be tortured and killed ourselves without question, but the animals? The Boxers had had a taste for dog someone claimed. But there weren't only dogs but cats, lizards, a parrot, a white rat, and a ferret under the tarpaulin. Sanitation had been the clincher. Barricaded in the hong we couldn't take the animals out to shit. But we weren't going to stay here long. Why not take the pets on the *Myrrha* with us when we escaped? The illogic, the mistake we'd made seemed dangerous. I couldn't figure out just how, because thinking about it now seemed dangerous, too.

The pallet came back. After loading the second dozen boxes, I knelt on the pallet myself. I hugged the blue pyramid and gripped the chains as tightly as I could. My weight made the pallet swing more when it was winched off the platform. The skin on my back crawled the whole ride down. Several times leaves hurtled through the air like green ribbons and stuck to the boxes or twined around the chains. Fussily I picked them off. They fluttered to the ocher water of the river.

MARK, ONE OF the hong's crew, was dying at that moment. He was the youngest, all I know. I was at the hong too short a time to befriend them, but I can still worry their names one by one, like a string of beads you fuss with to replace a worse habit. (More than that, I can imagine being them, being each one of them! Watch!) Now Mark was dead, or nearly so. The loss of blood, which was making his stomach cramp, also became a dizziness, a sort of drawn-out caper, but of a seriousness he'd have been quailing at were he more alert. The fear he felt was awful enough. He resisted falling asleep. An hallucinated swaddling of heavy furs around him wasn't getting any warmer. Just the opposite. He'd never fallen into a frigid sleep before, but he'd been in a cave once. He seemed to fall into a chasm like the cave he remembered. He would have writhed if not for the cold furs weighing so heavily on him. He wasn't sure exactly when he was awake. Time began to seem intermittent. Moments eternalized then ended suddenly the way they were supposed to.

Kirbie, the self-described medic, knelt over Mark and leaned on the two big wounds, diking the boy's life for a little while. Like an overturned tortoise, Mark rolled his head up off the floor whenever dozing threatened. Again and again he came to and whispered nonsense syllables. He whispered because vibration in his bone dry voicebox caused excruciating pain.

It had happened like this. Just before I hustled Old Ol out and ran upstairs to the ballroom to see to my treasure, a huge mob rushed the hong. One of the insurgents, crazed and probably drugged, got through the last of the unblocked hong doors. He shrieked weirdly after making it in, half-glorying in his obvious doom, and started flailing his machete. We had guns but hadn't had to use them yet. For a second, unnerved, we hesitated. Mark was hit by the blade. Fearful of shooting the boy, we waited until he was slashed again. Seymour fired. It took eight shots to bring the insurrectionist down. One hit Mark in the groin, but it didn't matter. Another .25 caliber ricochet hit Joe in the calf, a wound he didn't bother us with, or even mention. After a ninth, careful, slaughterhouse shot, we turned to Mark, who'd curled up apologetically nearby. I gestured to Ol and he and I went upstairs, leaving the others to deal with the wounded man. Or boy.

ON THE RIVERBOAT afterdeck the boxes' rope handles tugged at my arms like men on their deathbeds. My twenty-dollar boy sailor and I were relaying the boxes to the foot of a companionway. Next we'd haul them up to the cabin deck. Even lightly padded with oakum, the stacks of coins inside the boxes nodded against each other and made a dull clucking when moved. We looked up at the thump of a small explosion. The black wool of oil smoke, bolt upon bolt, fiddle-headed skyward from the hong next door, Cricket hong. The insurrectionists had set the place afire. From under the roar of the mob a rhythmic, toneless jangling could be heard. After I'd gone back to heaving boxes for a minute or two, I figured out the noise. They'd put a ram to the well-chained side gate of our own Bottom hong.

KIRBIE'S HANDS HAD gone stiff. Like two stumps of red coral they kept pressing on the sticky rags. In his heart he swore he'd never get angry or grouse about the faking, if the boy suddenly sprang up as sly ones sometimes did on the playing field, never letting on whether they'd really been hurt at all. The sweaty faces of those standing around skimmed what little light was in the dim room. They regarded Mark dolefully, stunned. Strong, hopeless hope made them wait for his eyes to flutter open one more time. After all, last night, one of the dogs—my own, in fact—had reawakened from carbon-monoxide slumber at the prick of the injection. He'd barked loudly, tried to bite the medic's hand. Sleep or death yanked his leash, and the bite became as dainty as a yawn falling closed. And what about Mark? His final stillness gripped them. When his jaw and wrists shuddered inhumanly, one or two of the men jumped. Kirbie raised his tortured hands.

It looked like a stylized gesture of horror or submission. In a single unpumped spate, blood spilled from under the rags.

They dragged Mark's body next to the insurrectionist's. Someone kicked the insurrectionist's leg to make room. A small gesture of hatred. But most of them were angry because, underneath it all, they sensed their feelings for the two bodies were about equal now. Yet each man, in his mind, still clamored for Mark. The boy might have been all-powerful like a hiding parent, though he'd always been the youngest, the cute, gullible one. Sailcloth was dropped over the remains.

COULD I HAVE LOVED them better than I did? I sized up the one I was with, my twenty-dollar sailor. His name was Topher Ammidon Smith. He wasn't one of the hong's crew. He belonged to the *Myrrha*. Though he had a guy-who-happens-to-be-around ordinariness, I still wondered whether I didn't love him more than anyone else in my life just then. For me there was a secret thread of hope and joy in our shared labor. A wild frisson started like the touch of ice cubes at my armpits when I thought that everything I'd ever thought about love was probably out-of-true.

Topher Ammidon Smith was young. He couldn't have been more than fifteen or sixteen. He'd let a smattering of whiskers grow long on his chin. And the blond prickling of a mustache didn't look virile so much as childishly vain. Still, he was big and might grow huge. His skin was sheet white, very strange in that climate. A healed break (I later learned) thickened the bridge of his nose, which gave him a slightly leonine air. In his short life

his body had sustained a lot of other damage. A V-shaped nick
was missing from the crest of a jug ear. A messy vaccination scar
was smeared on the skin of a man-sized shoulder. Another blurry
magenta scar ran from his chest's smattering of pimples to his
navel, which had the beard his elfin face couldn't grow. Even his
nails were damaged, bitten to stubs around which pillowed blush-
ing, gnawed-upon skin. His eyes, too, appeared damaged. Pale
blue, they had dark flaws like missing shards.

While I examined Topher, he was looking at the shore. Beyond
the godown was a walled courtyard. We couldn't see the jangling
gate but it was there. The mob was in an alley outside the gate.
There was another wall and another gate leading to the mirror
image courtyard of Cricket hong next door. The smoke from
Cricket was thinning and turning white. In vaporous gaps we
could see the mob flooding the hong yard over there. A trick of
the air made the smoke spiral up the huge mast that normally flew
the flag of the company, Matheson Dixwell, Inc.

"Holy . . ." Topher muttered. "They know what's going on
inside, you think? Should I run tell them?"

"They must've heard the explosion. They had to have looked
out, right?"

"They gotta know *Myrrha*'s fired up. What are they doing?" He
frowned as if trying to look through the walls of Bottom hong,
into the skulls of the funeral party inside.

"Everyone knows," I said. "They've known for a long time." I
wasn't sure they really knew we had to leave. They'd been told,
but it might not have sunk in. Mr. Haver, who wasn't that much
older than Topher, was in charge. He was the tyro with last night's

bright idea to kill the animals. Cooler heads—Kirbie, myself—
had fallen in line.

Now I shrugged. I shuffled a blue box toward the stacks at the
foot of the companionway. Before falling back to work, Topher
eyed the jumble of flimsy godowns along the river, built cheek by
jowl without alleys separating them. These were the weak points
of the hong defenses. If the insurrectionists went through the
godown, they could get from Cricket to Bottom without much
trouble. Maybe the fire was keeping them away. The river was
stripped of launches and skiffs. Boats of every kind had been taken
by people in flight. Otherwise we would have had to worry about
an attack from the water. But thinking was a waste of time. There
was no sense at all in the mob's actions. Topher and I kept moving
the boxes in relay. To the companionway, up the ladder-like stair,
him heaving from below with a soft grunting. From the head of
the companionway we'd then carry the boxes to my cabin door,
and into the tiny chamber.

IN BOTTOM HONG they began thinking about a plan of retreat.
(This isn't my imagination. It's certainty.) They came to the
idea of retreat reluctantly. They'd expected the insurrectionists
to be frustrated easily, changeable, liable to move on to simpler
destruction somewhere else. And, like me, they had loyalties to
their employers.

When the mob built a fire against the great wooden main doors
of the hong, the defenders were forced to send a runner with buckets to fetch river water so they could keep the wood doused or

flood the gaps. Unlike the group at the courtyard gate, the insur-rectionists at the main doors hadn't found anything to use as a ram. Sheer pressure of numbers probably could have breached the old brick walls, if not the doors, but the mob wasn't rational.

The man lowering buckets into the river was the first from inside to notice the attack on the side gate. He ignored the shout-ing of the *Myrrha*'s captain who was standing above him at the main deck railing of the riverboat. Bending over the last of my boxes, I could look along the railing and see the captain, an enormously fat man. Buttocks, armpits, inner thighs and back, his vast cream pants and white shirt had gone pinkish gray with sweat. He wore no epaulettes, cap, or insignia. Over the monotonous roar—his own red-faced screams, the wind, shouting from the hong, the mob, the throbbing of the *Myrrha*'s engine, and the similar hum of fire from Cricket hong—above all that, the one sound that grabbed me was the nervous, intimate scrabbling of the captain's rings on the painted pipe rail. He had four rings—plain gold, lapis, carnelian and a grille of tiny diamonds. I got a look at them much later. The aerial, metallic clicketing of the rings flew from bow to afterdeck and played in a fluttery, old-maidish rhythm in the pipe by my ear. Strange sound to come from the man mountain erupt-ing with abuse. The bucket carrier ignored him. When his buckets were full—it was Chris, I noticed—he went off at a waddling trot. The captain seemed to shrink slightly. Turning, he spotted me and pursed his mouth in a sort of greeting. His hands paddled at his hips in what looked like embarrassment, though he'd been yelling about a matter of life and death. *Get on board, or else . . .*

Chris soon returned with the buckets for more water. The

captain harangued him again, and again was ignored. Chris frowned with the effort of blocking out the fat man's screams. Then he ran from the godown to the hong at the peculiar gait that spared the silted water as much as possible. He must have warned them inside about the attack on the side gate, because when he got to the hong's back entrance two men had been stationed there, kneeling with rifles. They fired discouraging shots toward the gate, and for a while the battering stopped. Chris picked his way over their legs. The calves of their khaki pants became soaked with river water.

Chris felt a sort of joy when he was back inside the hong's dark lower room. (I know he did.) In the relative quiet, away from the fat captain, away from the mob, with most of the water still in his pails, a job well done, alive—for now. But he was frowning still. He'd told them about the attack on the side gate but hadn't mentioned the captain's hysterical ranting. This was a decision of significance he'd taken on himself. He thought about the decision, turning it in his mind like an *objet d'art*, again judging it the right one. It was somehow satisfying at any rate. Fuck the captain.

When Chris was definitely out of earshot, the captain wagged a pudgy hand in the air in disgust. The men with rifles couldn't hear any better. To the captain, it looked like the crew was now defending the hong, and only the hong—front and back entrances—but leaving the yard, the godown and the *Myrrha* unprotected. He took a step toward where I'd been standing on the afterdeck. I wasn't there anymore. Topher and I had gotten the boxes to the cabin deck. The captain meant to say something to me. (I know.) He wasn't sure what. He turned to the pilothouse instead.

The men with rifles took an occasional shot. Their eyes scanned
the walls, the gate, the godown, and what they could see of Cricket
hong next door, overrun. So they must have been the first to
notice an obscure figure rising out of the thinning smoke around
the huge mast in Cricket's yard. I'd just unlocked my cabin and
walked back along the passage to Topher and my piles of boxes.
Before starting on them, I went out to take a look at things from
the cabin deck rail. I also saw the figure rising, and recognized
him from his lavender shirt. His snakeskin belt was missing, a
fancy thing that would have caught a thieving eye.

Mr. Merriwether Hale, about twenty-two years old, had been
in training with Matheson Dixwell. I'd played cards with him and
a few of the hong's crew the night before last, losing $4.60. To ter-
rify us the insurrectionists had lashed his body to a spar and were
hauling it up the mast. His feet were bare (shoes stolen, too) and
bound together. His head drooped forward. It was hard to see,
but something horrible had been done to his face and hands. The
hitch on the spar was a bit off-center, so the awful cross leaned
to one side. Like the stevedore Kev's tiny gold cross when his
immense chest was tacky with sweat.

One of the men kneeling at the hong's back entrance fired
at the mast for some reason, maybe to ensure Hale was dead, a
wasted shot at that distance. The cross kept rising with a loath-
some stop-and-start, which set the bound legs swinging. Just
under the short topmast cross trees, where the company flag
would ordinarily fly, whatever tackle they'd used gave out under
the weight of a man and a good-sized spar. Trailing a hemp rib-
bon, the cross fell through the rag ends of smoke. Though the

insurrectionists roared like thunder and the spar snapped with a baritone report, my ear also picked out the higher-pitched crackling of Hale's bones—like dry leaves crumbled—just the way I'd earlier heard the bedizened captain's nervous tinkling of gold on painted brass.

Even after news of Hale's crucifixion got to them, the hong's crew remained tentative. What preoccupied the men was a safe in the hong and a strong room in the godown. Between them they held a treasure of U.S.$200,000 or more in gold. The steel-lined strong room was also packed with damask crepe dresses (which the local women prized) and lacquered tea caddies and blue-and-white dining sets (inferior copies of the Chinese pattern, but worth U.S.$16,000). Besides that, 125 pecolls of pepper and a quantity of sugar were still in storage in the godown. Two days earlier the last tea boat had passed. It was nudged gingerly along the very narrow channel open to vessels of its draft this far up the river. I'd mentioned twice to Mr. Haver, once to several of the others, that it was probably in their interests to hire space aboard it. I didn't myself only because I'd already booked on the nimbler, safer *Myrrha*. All I got were shrugs. Mr. Haver explicitly demurred.

Even now, nerves pulped, Mr. Haver and the crew somehow dreamed the mob would be drawn off. Perhaps the so-called Mandarins—from pure contempt, they liked to call them the "Mandaroons"—perhaps they'd order their vaunted guards to the river. In that dark lower room of the hong, the twin sailcloth-covered bodies, Mark's and the crazed insurrectionist's, somehow emitted a narcotic air that had nothing to do with their unplaceable smell, too faint to be revolting. (I smell it now! I may as well be there!) After rushed prayers the crew had scattered to the room's corners. Now they stood inactive, strategically lethargic, though each was also alert, too alert in a way. They'd splashed the doors with river water. They could hear a monotonous clip-clopping as barrel staves were tossed into a pyre against the doors, and they heard the tinkling scrapes of broken glass scuffed aside. Last night, right after the slaughter of the animals, Mr. Haver had ordered bottles smashed at every entrance to the hong. He'd imagined the insurrectionists, if they attacked at all, would do it by stealth.

Now the hong's men kept glancing at him. And at the covered bodies. If he didn't say a word soon, they looked as if they might give in to complete paralysis. Or rout. So Mr. Haver spoke up. He decided it was time to get the hong's treasure on to the *Myrrha*. Only one of their boxes was ever loaded.

THE *MYRRHA*, AS the *Rose of Khartoum*, had belonged to the Sudanese government railway authority before she was transported to B. Of very shallow draft she had no holds to speak of, but pen-like arrangements for carrying cargo, or sheep or bullock, on the open main deck. A boxy two-deck superstructure had been built to accommodate large numbers of passengers on mahogany benches. The benches had been junked and the lower, longer deck converted into rudimentary cabins aft of the engine and boiler room. Forward, just behind the pilothouse, a spacious strong room had been outfitted for transferring invoices and treasure among the local warehouses and to the capital, A, a seaport fifty miles downriver.

For this run the strong room was going to serve as a kind of dormitory for last-minute passengers—the hong's crew, it went without saying, though they'd never booked. The strong room wouldn't be comfortable. The *Myrrha*'s aging side lever engine expended more than a few of its three-hundred horsepower just to heat the windowless room and to set it vibrating.

The open-sided top deck, indeed every cranny of the *Myrrha*, was usually jammed with passengers clutching leashed monkeys, mysteriously shapeless bundles or caged fowl. Often the captain had to order loafers, or whole contented families, off of the flimsy triangular spurs of the paddle box called paddle walks. People liked to lounge on them, because the revolving floats cast a cool, watery breeze through the paddle box vents. On an earlier short trip I'd found a companionway ladder to the top deck hung all over with dried leaves and clusters of wrinkled, tawny berries, which someone was hoping to sell in A. On each pierced-metal step with its fringe of medicine, an identical malnourished child had perched zigzag fashion, some drowsy, some observant as lemur. For this run, there were no local passengers, few passengers of any kind. The upper deck was empty. It was too exposed to sniper fire from the shores.

After getting all my boxes to the cabin deck, my twenty-dollar sailor Topher and I pushed them one by one along the tongue-and-grooved floor of the passage. Topher went almost to his hands and knees to shove. His blond brows dipped, and pearls of sweat fell to the bridge of his nose. When the spot tickled, he rubbed it, and the box he was still pushing veered left into the bulkhead. He laughed and collapsed to the floor. He glanced at me as if we were just two men working together. As if he hadn't been paid.

In fact, paying him had been tricky. I'd run into him two nights before, coming back from Cricket and my poker loss. I spotted him under a lantern on the dock, worrying a sore on his elbow with licked fingers, because he couldn't reach it with his tongue, though he tried. I invited him into a shed attached to the godown, and we sat at a zinc table over two tin cups of coffee dosed with rum. Despite being $4.60 poorer, I was willing to spend a lot more to guarantee a helper's devotion. Even though Mr. Haver and the hong's crew seemed oblivious and had let the tea boat leave that noon high in the water, I knew something awful was in the air. I'd already booked out on the *Myrrha*.

Over the spiked coffee I explained to Topher that I was going to need help with my cargo. I pronounced "help" strangely, since it was hard asking for anything even when money would smooth the way. I couldn't get "help me" to sound desirable or natural. I made it sound like indenture or something awful. He shrugged and seemed to think the whole conversation unnecessary. He worked for the captain, I was a passenger, of course he'd help me. I took a different tack. I asked him where he came from.

Easy as opening an unlocked door. He talked for an hour. At one point in the course of his story I laid the twenty-dollar gold piece on the table with a murmur. No explanation. His shattered blue eyes rolled down to it with faint equine alarm but he went on talking without interruption. A terrible story about a father, curdled by life, for whom he'd kept house and cooked, by whom he'd been locked in a half basement and beaten up "more than average," and whom he'd finally escaped at fourteen. The story had a tale-teller's roundedness, which made it a little difficult to credit every detail. Not that there was any question of deceit. In fact, mixed with his evident pride in the polish and eventfulness of his life's story was genuine sorrow. His lower eyelids crept up with recollected emotion only to drop and rise differently with a confiding, almost commercial smile, then drop a third time into an expression beautiful for not having any intention I could guess, just an unselfconscious and perfectly vulnerable laxness.

His hands gripped his bare shoulders and slid down to his elbows. With naïve sensuality he petted himself as he went on talking. He seemed to have forgotten about the twenty dollars lying on the table, except he glanced at the coin once or twice. I wasn't sure whether it was the money or his tale-teller's sentimentality or the coffee and grog that made the way he spoke a little quirky: he'd half swallow his voice, a sound like a nightingale's glub-glub, when he came to certain powerful words like "respect," "father," "promise," "do my best."

When we stood up, the coin remained untouched. "Don't forget," I ordered gently, hardly glancing at it. "You've got to take it. I truly need your help." His hand floated over the table. I turned my head away. I heard the sound—like any metals at all—of gold sliding briefly over zinc. Behind me, his deepest, softest voice came. "Thank you. Thank you."

I WAS ALONE in my cabin with my boxes. Now came a wait. It seemed long. I couldn't move in the tiny space without climbing over boxes. For a minute I sat in a pinching chair of boxes, my feet resting on more boxes. Fitfully, I curled up on the bed's thin

green coverlet. My clothes were soaked with sweat. My muscles
trembled when I moved. Even when I was still they quivered,
unless I held my limbs just so. My heart raced. I had trouble
breathing in the heat. Sweat made for an intriguing tear-like con-
coction around my eyes. The more I relaxed the more my body
was pestered by itches, twitches and tingling, like the creakings
and pings of an engine when it shuts down. I had to shift to my
back to breathe. I reached up to open the window. The glass was
cloudy, and the all over coal smoke and yellowish smudge was
spotted by past rain. No rain had come today.

With work finished, I seemed to give out beneath myself like
worn cloth. I fell through to a lower level of existence where I
wasn't an actor at all. This level of existence was a room identical
to my cabin. I was senses, nothing more. I heard—despite the
noise still raging outside—the soft clunk of a chair or a chest or
a box and the surprisingly light, clear report of a cough. B's last
rich escapees seemed to be reading patiently in the cabins around
mine. Rather than replay the too-fresh horror of Hale's cross in
my mind's eye, the usual loop ran—what I saw whenever my eyes
closed and thought flagged was the "Langlais" brothers beating
Clancy Rasmussen to death with two of the bars used to hang
copper pots on, pot hooks still attached. I opened my eyes. I probably looked calm—as I had when it happened, watching the scene
from several miles journey behind my own face. A more terrible
journey than people imagine. What do they call it? *Sangfroid*.

Ordinarily the captain would only pay his respects to actual shippers or company officials. I thought he might come to me, a sort
of supercargo, because he'd want to know what the hong's crew

were thinking, information he'd expect me to have. He'd seen I
was aboard earlier. Even as I lay there trying to be calm, I expected
to be interrupted. I twiddled a five-dollar coin in my pocket. It
didn't matter, because I was terribly startled when the captain did
knock. I leapt up. I got the coin into his sweaty palm, thanking him
for Topher's service. Startled himself, he looked down at the coin
before his expression cleared and he murmured hoarsely, "Kind of
you. Generous." His gaze danced curiously over the blue boxes. I
could tell he disliked me, but I couldn't guess why.

"I think they're hoping the mob will pass farther along the hong
road, if they can just hold out a little longer," I explained. "They
might even still be thinking the Mandarins will get involved—"
The captain snorted. "—They've been talking about it nonstop
for days."

The man immediately began raging as if I weren't present.
To nurse his slightly artificial fury he avoided looking at me. "It's
intolerable. He won't even—he was pretending not to hear me,
that . . . I have no idea what they expect of me. I *will* leave. I've
told them that." He stole a surprisingly dainty glance to see how
I was reacting.

"Did you put up the—what is it?—blue peter? The flag?"

He sighed as if the question were irrelevant. "We don't use it on
the river. We have a steam whistle." His rings flickered dismissively.
Fixing his gaze on—I think—my crotch he started fuming again.
"And I did. Hours ago I was blasting it. They begged me to stop."

I tried to remember. "The other passengers? How are they?"

"What? Very stoical. Oh, there's been a word or two. A nervous word or two. Some helped us set up cots, and that without a

single please or thank-you from those—" Massaging his temples he bucked his head backward to mean the men in the hong.

"I think they're completely stunned. This didn't happen the way they expected. And Mr. Haver's too young, or he just doesn't have the right character—"

"That's it!" the captain yelled at the boxes over my shoulder. "It's a matter of leadership. I am the leader aboard this ship. Those men—these are conditions of warfare. This is not a—a—" he sneered, "*commercial*—lah-di-dah walk in the park! They have no notion of military . . . I have one and only one duty, and that's to my passengers—I won't say *especially* to the ones who bothered to book passage!" He caught my eye and amended in a soft voice, "Given the circumstances, obviously . . ."

"Have they even started loading—?"

"One box, one box!" he interrupted. "And you know . . . at this point . . ." He looked up and down the corridor. He was far too fat to enter the room, even to pass through the door. I had one knee on boxes, one foot on the floor. The captain stood outside holding the thin cabin door with his left hand and fanning it nervously. "I'm almost—*almost*—worried that if I did sound the whistle again, they'd react rashly. You know what they're like."

"What? They'd try to stop us?" It was a wild idea, but was it plausible? I had to consider it for a moment, think of the personalities involved.

The captain didn't say anything. Then in a semi-hysterical tone of voice, as if there hadn't just been a long pause, he glanced at the doorjamb, "Who knows?! Who knows?! Mr. Haver is a little boy, as you said. The pressure . . ."

"Only one box. They'll never have time to get all the——"

"Without doubt! They can't still be thinking . . . We leave now!"

"You're ready this minute?"

"I have been for hours," he said contemptuously. More cajoling: "Oiler, stoker on the job. And Topher, too, now that he's finished with your . . . My crew and passengers are all aboard. That's it."

"Could we send—or, better, you go yourself? Explain. I don't know the situation at the front doors, but the side gate isn't going to hold much longer. Do they realize? They must."

"Of course they do. They've lost their minds. Suicidal heroism. Just what a little boy dreams of."

"If you——"

"Could I make it across the yard?!" He looked at me witheringly, making a gesture to remind me of his bulk. "A captain can't leave his vessel under these——" he added primly, sounding as if the argument had just occurred to him. "And what if they broke through and I was blocked in the hong, what then? My boy's no pilot yet."

"When they come back with more boxes to load, we can . . . Or Ol can go back inside now and get them."

"They won't listen." He eyed me and began, "Unless you tell me they're on their way . . ."

At this juncture maybe I was supposed to offer to go myself. But I couldn't possibly leave my boxes. Among all the other risks, I now wondered whether the captain had guessed what was inside them. I pressed my knee against the box lid it rested on. The knowing way he looked at me made this pause especially uncomfortable. His somewhat feminine lips compressed, decolored, vanished. He was staring over my shoulder but I could imagine he was angry at me. It didn't seem fair.

He wasn't really angry, or not at me. "Unless you tell me they're on their way—were on their way when you were coming out . . ." the captain repeated. He barked and pounded the doorjamb with his fist. "What else is there to do? We understand each other." This last wasn't exactly a question.

I didn't answer. I shook my head gravely. "The atmosphere in there was—they're panicking. They don't know what they're doing. A boy was killed. And with what just happened next door at Cricket . . . I think we're all panicking." It scared me to think this might be true. I made a shameful argument. "They won't listen to me either. Or Mr. Haver definitely won't. I told them two days ago they'd better load their cargo on the tea boat that came through." I sounded defensive, and I knew I shouldn't have to defend myself. I eyed the captain suspiciously as if he'd turned the tables on me somehow. Had the scene been prepared? But he was looking at the boxes under my knee and clearly not thinking about me at all. He appeared determined to remain at just the right pitch of anger. I repeated, "I think we're all panicking. All of us."

"This isn't panic. This is coherent," the captain said, narrowing his eyes to look daggers at the boxes. "Could they be stalling? Loading especially slowly?"

"No. Not now. Not at this stage," I answered. I went back to the earlier point. "This isn't *panic* panic we're feeling, but panic in the sense of—"

"Us? You and me?" He looked at me. "I think this is coherent. I think we're being clear. We understand each other. I have my duty. You clearly have your . . ." He was looking at the boxes, referring to them, but thinking of something else. "I know it's an awful . . ."

"Our positions aren't equivalent. *Are* we being clear?" I really wondered.

"Very clear, I think."

"No, we're not." Unlike myself, I stumbled. "I don't think . . ."

"I'm perfectly coherent. Aren't you? There are indeed no options. Not a one."

"Let's blow the whistle again."

"The whistle," he said bitterly.

"Or both of us try calling to them." I blushed. "Both of us," I insisted despite my embarrassment, which was making me feel almost light-headed, as though the blush were siphoning the blood from my heart.

"Both of us," he repeated in the same unpleasant tone of voice.

"Stop parroting me!" I snapped. My anger amazed me. As if the universal violence had glittered through the narrowest human chink—me!—the last shadow in an all-consuming blaze of passion. I softened, "I'm not sure we *are* being clear." That wasn't exactly true. I was sure we were being clear *and at the same time* sure we weren't. The effect was like stupidity or being out-of-true, rather than like real doubt.

"Clear, clear, clear, clear, clear," the captain sang irritably and was interrupted by a rafale of gunfire from shore. Scowling, avoiding my eyes, he took it as an excuse to leave. I made my way to the cabin deck rail just to make sure the side gate hadn't been over-run. The men were still positioned at the back entrance to the hong, so the gate held. My other eye kept a clear view down the passage to my cabin door. No one went near it until I re-entered a moment later.

Soon after that, when I was hunched on the bed swallowing bile and worrying the bruises on my ankles and shins, I heard the *Myrrha*'s engine change register, felt it through muscle and bone. There were some shufflings-about in the cabins around mine. Hawsers hit the lower deck. The usual shouts came faintly through the general noise. The wheel splashed into motion. The whistle didn't sound. When the *Myrrha* moved I could feel the turbulent fluid in me wash a little back toward shore.

I thought I'd have some peace. Not peace exactly but the nothingness of being alone. An awkward shambling in the passage jerked me back to the normal level of existence. My name was called several times in a hoarse whisper. I knew who it was. With surprising readiness I wiped my face and pulled my sweat-damp pants loose on my legs. I smoothed my hair. I only noticed how anxious I was, deep down, because my heartbeat had spun up.

Ol, the donkey engine operator, was out in the passage, the only one of the hong's crew aboard. He looked a little drunk already, and his face had the elevated, demented alertness a drunk's often does. Seeing his pop-eyed expression I felt two black waves of emotion. First, grief. Sometimes it takes seeing another person to make something, even something you're part of yourself, come clear. Second, anger at Ol, the captain and myself. We seemed worthless. I could tell just by looking at him that Ol was going to argue, but not so hard he'd risk the *Myrrha* turning back.

He staggered up to me. Too close. His filthy hands rose, but he didn't dare touch me. His rag of a shirt was open all the way down, and he pressed his hands to his chest in a sort of pleading gesture. He was trying to look angry but couldn't manage stronger than quizzical. He rubbed that nose of his, which looked like it had joints, if no muscles. He must have been sixty, twice my age, but was utterly servile. He was stammering.

"What is it?"

"But Christ, you didn't hear! We're going and we——" He started hacking.

"Of course, I heard." My expression was hard. What was I supposed to say? It was too bad? I was sorry? I hadn't been clear enough?

His face glimmered at me out of the dimness with a sort of emotional opalescence. Obviously coldheartedness wasn't the reaction he'd expected. "Ah, my God A'mighty, my God A'mighty, my God A'mighty," he said, his voice plaintive. He moaned. "You don't see anything wrong?"

"Of course, I do," I said. "You tell me what we should do?" That was cruel, asking him like that, a man who'd never made a decision in his life. But I only had misery to spread around just then.

Ol was stymied. Then he whispered, "Fucking Mandaroons." That was followed by a sob. He pressed his forehead against the bulkhead. I closed my eyes at the sight of his yellow-crusted ear, wiry with grizzled hairs. "I'm all alone in there. Nobody but me." He meant in the strong room. "There's cots set up for the boys, see? And there's nobody but me. And it's hot as hell."

"So you're alone. What are you asking me?" I said remorselessly.

"Where are they? That's the question. There's cots, see? But where are they?"

"Ol, I know that. I know what you're saying. I feel the same way you do." I was softening and it hurt.

"Why didn't they get on?" he moaned. Not "why did we leave?" I couldn't help noticing. The same way he'd been happy enough to light out of the lower room with me after Mark was wounded.

"Look, we know they're—they're well armed. And they're able to think and plan. Unlike the mob. Maybe, after all, the Mandarins . . ."

He looked at me as if I'd betrayed him, just when I'd broken down and was trying to comfort him. His fingers, horny and yellow as parsnips, drew a circle on his chest, which was nearly muddy with sweat and grime. Though we'd only known each other a few days, he then said something strange, before a fit of hacking got to him and he turned his back on me: "I always hated you."

"We don't know what's going to happen," I told him as he walked away. He listed against the bulkhead but didn't turn back.

"We know!" he crowed after a long while, from a long way off.

3

EVENING. THE CALLS of monkeys, birds and insects overwhelmed the river. A few sustained, expressive yelps streamered
over the rest, but mostly it was the rhythmic, rising and decaying
roar of a million rudimentary languages. They were easy enough
to understand: a numbingly contradictory chorus of *Here I am!*
and *Come to me!* and *Go away!* The aerial noise saturated my
mind, becoming as identical to the night as the darkness was.
But now I seem able to see and hear everything, to separate out
every detail . . .

HERE WAS THE CAPTAIN. A man made up of a hundred con-
vexities, some shadowed with sweat, some sagging or bulging as

he breathed, he almost filled a specially-built coir-padded cubby in the pilothouse. His stertor may have been the most ambiguous sound on the whole droning river. The riverboat lights were slightly dimmed by dark flurries of what looked like animated jungle litter. And even the tiny light in the pilothouse precipitated the occasional green flying thing from the darkness outside. Unimpressed by magical-seeming photocatalysis, the captain now and then brushed these bits of twiggy life from the mounds of his shoulders or belly, his beringed hand moving with lethargic insensitivity.

He'd started out as a librarian in the much colder climate where he was born and raised. The key to his few, rather formal, friendships of the time, had been his labored-over skill with an anecdote. He had a remote, well-ordered, polysyllabic way of speaking, which he considered amusing as well as impressive. He was less talented at give-and-take and argument. Early on, before he could even be said to have had one, he let obesity cut him off from sexual life. He started a huge collection of erotic studio photographs. He lived alone and used to come home from the library to regale himself with port, whiskey and expensive cheeses as he catalogued his collection. It was ordered strictly chronologically. He liked the perversity of imposing a notion of history on sex. These evenings he'd often spiral into the untethered, maybe unreal, giddiness that comes out of solitary, self-indulgent contentment. And just as often he'd crash.

If an erection formed—he had his desires—he had a neat trick. Flecked with crumbs of cheese, amber-spotted with whiskey, he'd lean back in his huge chair. The erection had formed within the folds of himself, and he had the incredible ability to finish it off with a steady, rhythmic motion of his body in the chair. His hands, in archival cotton gloves, never touched his body, and he remained clothed. While he fixed dinner afterward, the fluid between his skin and clothing dried and began to flake away like dandruff. Much later the last of it washed off when he lumbered into his evening shower. Though he lived like an old man, he was only twenty-five at the time.

Later, he became secretary of a yacht club. Trying to emulate the rich members, he moved to Antigua briefly. There, he befriended a very ugly but kind, sober Great Lakes ore boat captain, who vacationed on the island. They set up house together near Detroit. They soon returned to the tropics. The ore boat captain was old. He decided on B, switching from tricky ore boats on lake waves like rabbit punches to a drowsy side-wheeler on a river exactly like sleep. From taciturnity the ugly older man slipped into death. The new captain employed his inheritance, the *Myrrha*, more and more depressively. He could hardly rouse himself from deep sorrow in life to marvel at finding himself where he was, in command, in graceful, dreamlike motion on the weird river. In his cubby, he heaved shallow breath upon breath and glowered at the black water.

HALF A MILE behind us torches were lit on the broken-down, highly ornamented pier of Sultan Rapithwin's mausoleum. The funerary knoll was surmounted by a radio tower with a beacon blinking red at the top. Who knows what the beacon warned away? Apart from a single, just-arrived fleet of helicopters, there were no airfields and no air traffic in the country and never had been.

"It's more powerful than the government radio station, you know. They hate that in the capital. It was funded by Rapithwinists from overseas," the shadow next to me began speaking energetically. "That's why they stopped letting funding come in for them. Pure jealousy. Though maybe there's some truth them saying the Rapithwinists were passing some of their loot along to the insurrection. Who knows, really?"

"You're working for one of the companies? Or a reporter?" I asked. I'd come to a spot on the rear deck where I could look out and still keep an eye on my cabin door along the corridor inside.

He laughed. He made a self-deprecating joke, avoiding specifics. "Oh, a bit of an academic, bit of a journalist, bit of a ne'er-do-well." He chuckled on, and a small eddy from the floats chuckled against the *Myrrha*'s hull in response. "Yeah, who knows?" He sighed. "I guess I should be a reporter. I've been here long enough trying to figure things out. Like that radio tower there—" He pointed. "I know the government wants to take it down—or take it over probably—but the companies won't let them. It's childish, really. Government's convinced they're sending secret messages in all that religious babble. The companies are sensitive, because the radio is a big part of the religion, believe it or not. Do you know about them? I don't want to bore you."

"No, go on. I don't know a thing about them."

"Well, that's why they put it on his grave. Somehow he's supposed to be talking to them through the radio signal. Or they turn into radiation when they die. It's pretty weird, but basically a cargo cult—I mean, that level of sophistication." He cocked his head and decided. "No, maybe more than that, because there's the old Islam connection and all the spooky physics business."

"Who are they? The Kara-kara?"

"Karak's more polite. No, there're almost no Indian Rapithwinists. They're mixed race mostly. An old Portuguese community that went native. Then Islam came in—I'm not sure, eighteenth century, I guess—but it was always coastal. By then the Mandarins were running things, just like the companies now, and they got forced upriver. Then everything was screwed up with independence." He pretended to look at me for the first time. "I'm Carter Van Loon, by the way. Probably never heard of him, but there was a famous geographer named Van Loon. Ancestor of mine, same family. What are you up to down here?"

"Supercargo."

"Yeah? What ship? Who with? Anders Willis back at Bottom?"

"Oh, not one of the big companies. I was on the *Clay*, working for a consortium. Not local. Bunch of speculators, really."

"Mm. Bad timing."

I shrugged.

"Really bad," he insisted. "That was horrible back there. I saw some terrible things."

"What? At the hong? Or at Cricket?"

"Well, they were fighting there too, I guess, right before we left. I meant last night. The consulate. Or even before I ended up at the consulate. I was at the executions. That's where it started, you know. Beheadings. This day and age and they're still chopping people's heads off. You ever seen that?"

"No. I didn't know how it started."

"Well, of course it was going to happen anyway. It was simmering all along. But the big mobs started with the executions. I'm amazed the companies let the Mandarins get away with it. I guess I should feel grateful, since they were the ones protecting the consulate. And they brought us all down to the hong in a van this morning. Still . . . You were at the hong?"

"Mm."

"What was that like?"

"Last night?"

"Yeah. And today."

"Well. Last night was weird. We knew it had started, and there were only a few of us in the place. Then today a kid was killed. They rushed the place."

"Shit."

"Yeah. We were basically besieged. But you must have seen what happened today."

"Not really. I mean, I knew they were attacking, but I slept mostly." He laughed sheepishly. "I was up all night. Someone said they overran the hong next door, Matheson Dixwell's place."

"That's Cricket, yeah. Some guys got killed there, too."

"It was inevitable. I mean, the whole fucking thing was inevitable."

"I think they probably overran our place in the end. Not 'ours' but the one I was at. Bottom. Anders Willis had some guys there. They were supposed to come with us."

"No shit?" Van Loon looked into the black braids of water trailing the riverboat. He murmured "shit" again with an oddly formal, valedictory intonation. But I figured the real story was eluding him, like the boat's wake. "They didn't make it, huh?"

"No," I confirmed.

"You'll have to tell me what happened. Sit down and tell me the whole thing. It's the Mandarins' fault. That's what we were all saying at the consulate. They decided they were just going to defend the city center and their little stretch of the riverfront. They wrote off the hongs, basically said 'fuck you.' It's resentment against the companies."

"Understandable," I whispered. "Not just the Mandarins. The whole country. The people, they must hate the companies."

"There's really no 'people,'" Van Loon assured me. "But if you want to use that term for your average powerless schlub, then for the *people* it's about supporting whoever pays them a little money and doesn't kill too many of them too often. That's the companies, it turns out. So the *people* probably resent the companies less than they do the power blocs. It's sick, and it'll be a mess in the long run, but . . . "

"What do you mean, there's no people?"

"Who are the people? The Karak, the Mandarins, the Rapithwinists, the urban Marxists, the army, the companies' local employees, the little opposition groups, this or that group wandering around the jungle from a couple of wars ago (those are the ones terrorizing the Karak)?" Van Loon ticked off the list glibly. He made even the chaos of the country sound neatly organized, the way a journalist would. I knew it wasn't like that. I knew the Mandarins were collapsing. Edge bled into edge, and there was no center. "Or is the government the people? That's a joke. They're the weakest and most irrelevant piece of the puzzle."

Van Loon seemed to like my good-student silence. He went on for a long time about the unfathomable situation in the country. I leaned back against the railing, looking down the corridor inside the riverboat, wondering what I could do with my treasure. Overhead sparks kept spiraling up out of the stacks along with black smoke. Every so often actual flame shot up, which illuminated the roiling, serpentine clouds that ran leeward. In the flash of satanic lightning you could glimpse the glassy black water and the infinite creaming wake of the wheel. Even leaves of the jungle gleamed red.

One of the crewmen came and announced the captain had asked to see me. I wondered about this summons but was tired of listening to Van Loon at that point. "I really do want to sit down with you. Talk about what happened," he called into the corridor after me.

I grunted insincerely.

I told the crewman that I'd come along in a minute. I wasn't sure I would. It would mean leaving my boxes unguarded. In my cabin I sat atop them debating with myself for a long time. I weighed the reassuring thought that, even if someone broke into the cabin, they couldn't get any boxes off the riverboat while it was en route.

In the end, remembering my earlier conversation with the captain, I was too curious not to go. But I was careful. I secured the sticking window's brass screw locks. I scanned the room. I tested a soft-looking spot on the wall with my fingers. A bubble of nicotine-stained paint shattered, showing solid, heavy wood underneath. I crawled out over the boxes and locked the door. I tried the unfamiliar latch three times to make sure. I wouldn't be gone long.

WHEN I ENTERED the pilothouse, the captain was lounging in his cubby instructing a boy at the helm. The boy turned and chucked his head at me in greeting. It was my twenty-dollar sailor, Topher Ammidon Smith. He looked back at the river ahead of us. He ruffled the fingers of his smudged white hands which had too tight a grip on the wheel. He did it several times—beautiful motion!

The captain was saying, "Right there is Rapithwin's first pier. One they never finished building. When you're abreast it you right-rudder—*now*—slowly $036\frac{1}{2}°$ so you're heading on the Slump Island range lights. See! In the daylight there's a white high-rise behind them, a lot of balconies."

"I see it."

"Good night vision," the captain muttered. "No electricity. It was a scam them putting it up here in the middle of nowhere. Jungle. Kara-kara think it's haunted." In a firm but surprisingly affectionate voice, he went on. "You go two-and-three-quarters miles here. It's best to stay a bit to the left of the range line, because the current pushes you west."

There was a box at the captain's feet. It was smaller than my own. "Anders Willis" was stenciled on one end and also inked in a calligraphic hand on a label on top. The nails of the lid had been sprung and the lid carefully replaced. "What have you got?" I asked. Not brightly but with dark needling.

Though neither of us looked at the box, the captain knew what I was talking about. "Whether I've 'got' it will have to wait," he huffed. "I haven't *got* anything. *I* haven't got anything, I should say."

"The box from Bottom hong. That's it? All they got out?" "Turned out to contain papers mostly. Some silver coins. Petty cash, maybe."

"Strange to start with that."

"I didn't examine the papers. They could be important." He was irritated with me for beginning on this so quickly.

I was only a little suspicious of the captain at this point. I became much more so later. After all, the hong crew told me they had gold. Why not start with that? For now, I teased the fat man. "Looks like you've made it part of your hoard." Besides the box at his feet, a bulky loose-leaf binder of sailing directions, a half-crushed box of Kleenex and some paperbacks cluttered his little cubby. I meant he looked like an ogre sitting there surrounded by his possessions. Topher seemed to get the pale joke and chuckled softly.

The captain wasn't bothered in the least. He smiled. "Oh, please. You think I'm absconding with their things? Naturally, I put everything that was in the box in the *Myrrha*'s safe. Only place for it." He scooted an inch or two forward and leaned over with some grunting. The coir shifted under him. His bald forearm reached out. He lifted the well-sanded lid of the Anders Willis box. Inside were blackened rags and several plastic bottles. I eyed the gleaming brass everywhere in the pilothouse and the pasty streaks of tarnish on Topher's hands and understood. The way the captain had raised the lid with a mincing "*voilà*" had a note of drama, which I could see by his own expression displeased him now. Smirking without humor, he said, "In this country you learn to let nothing go to waste. I did exactly what was proper. The box wouldn't fit in the safe. I figured we could use it."

"Oh, that's right, the strong room isn't free this run. Or is it?"

He didn't answer. I couldn't help thinking how strange it was he'd ordered the boy to polish brass after all we'd been through that day. I was silent, eyeing Topher, to be honest. Wondering how much he knew, but also, at a lower level of existence, just looking. I don't know why. He absorbed me.

The captain was a self-conscious man, definitely intelligent. He was still dwelling on the box, feeling slightly foolish or exposed after insisting on its contents. Playing at small talk, he said, "No. Upkeep is Sisyphean in this climate. Upkeep of anything, oneself included. Ha ha." No one laughed. "Topher here nearly died of a cut on his thumb. No?"

"Right," the boy said. Belatedly he laughed a note or two, but he was concentrating nervously on steering the boat.

Something tickled the back of my neck. I spasmed, slapped it. Even Topher glanced back. I was on edge.

The captain said, "We were under enormous pressure back there." He gave a long, sticky cough and swallowed. "They have an office—of course, it's the main one, headquarters—Anders Willis does, in A." He was sidling toward the issue at hand. "And I thought in the end I'd turn over the papers and silver to them and just explain what happened." He thought for a moment about how that sounded. "Goes without saying, I suppose. It was my intention anyway." He frowned at himself. "There was such a hullabaloo back there, I really don't know what you . . ." He was going to say "thought" but trailed off and pretended to be occupied shifting his possessions around him.

I gathered he was conferring with me, hoping our memories would jibe, and if not, intending to make the little touch-ups that come so easily after confusing events.

"When we decided, you and I . . ." he began, testing out the sound of that on me. *We* decided to cut out! "Sit down! Sit down!" Ruffling his jowls amiably he nodded at a stool just behind Topher. I couldn't sit on it without pressing up against the boy. I shook my head and remained by the door. My treasure preoccupied me, and I wanted to keep the interview short. In my pocket I pushed my forefingertip's pillow of flesh into the cabin key's brazen loop. I felt a general resistance to the captain. I must have mistrusted him a little.

"Such a tragedy . . ." the fat man murmured. Then, launching into the main business, he began, "It's awkward for me, if you thought when you gave me that very generous pourboire, the—uh—five-dollar piece . . ." I saw the tendons rise on the backs of Topher's hands and wondered whether he'd mentioned the twenty I gave him. "If you thought I was accepting it as some special . . . recognition having to do with this particular occasion. For instance, thanks for, perhaps, having hastened our departure in a tense situation . . ." He quickly added "or . . ." with a big show of thought, just to slow me down.

"I remember you were shrieking your head off," I said. Topher almost laughed. "I don't think you needed me to hurry us up."

When Topher made the sound of mirth this time, the captain's face went suddenly blank with suspicion. I could see his surprise. He looked from me to Topher. I could almost see him register in an instant the total time I'd spent eyeing the boy since coming to the pilothouse. It wasn't something I wanted him thinking about. Anyway, he had more urgent business to discuss with me. He seemed to file a thought away. Even the rings under his eyes were somehow convex, udder-like. He drew them up and continued, looking at me narrowly.

"Yes, I was angry. Turns out I was right to be. Unfortunately. But what I was saying . . . You saw how distracted I was when I took the coin. To be honest, that was because I thought it was a dollar at most. And a small tip like that is perfectly ordinary— not strictly condoned but nothing unusual when a special cabin is requested, for example, or . . ."

"Condoned? Are you not a private operator? You're not, are you?"

"No, no, the *Myrrha's* under contract with the government, as a matter of fact," he said lightly. "Problem of day-to-day expenses, after my dear friend, the late captain passed away."

"I understand." I added, "Clear." That was just an echo, neither needling nor a joke.

"Or . . . or . . ." the captain was saying. "Or when we have a delay because of some tricky quayside procedure. People will tip in a case like that. Well, a case like your loading your boxes from the godown gantry, now that I think about it. That did cause us a long wait."

"I loaded from the hong directly." I was contradicting an irrel-evant detail. My resistance to him kept flaring up.

"Or from the hong. That's what I meant. Of course."

I didn't understand where the captain was headed. It made me nervous, as if I risked being outmaneuvered. It didn't seem he was chiefly worried about leaving men to die. Apparently a tiny problem of financial ethics loomed larger for him. Could it be like that in this country? Deciding to let him off the hook, I shrugged. "Well, I gave it to you for Topher. That's all. A simple thing."

The captain looked embarrassed. As if he'd been caught appropriating someone else's money. "Oh, it wasn't for . . . " A finger touched one of the mounds of his chest.

I almost laughed. "No, it was. I was thanking you for loaning me Topher's services. He was a huge help to me."

That made the captain happy. "Of course. That's perfectly reasonable. And—you hear that Topher?—and I will give him —something."

"It wasn't a lot, considering," I said. I came in and sat on the stool finally, bumping against Topher companionably, making myself at home as a subtle dig at the captain. I'd decided that, at the normal level of existence, it would be smart to appease him. "Sorry," I muttered to the boy, who casually shifted so it was more his hip than his butt pressing against my side. Maybe I could have given him more room. "Cramped," I said gruffly, making it sound like a real complaint. But all my attention had drained to the deepest part of me to concentrate on the faint warmth of the small part of his body in contact with mine.

"Topher, do you have to stick your bottom in the poor man's face?" the captain snapped.

Topher laughed with good humor. "What am I supposed to do

with it?" He arched his lower back sharply and wiggled his butt at us. "Forget boxes, I oughta start charging to get close to this baby." He gave it a whack. "Feast your eyes, guys."

I laughed. The kid's cheery vulgarity surprised me a little. His being sentimental had made me think he was shy, too. I gave him more room, slid half off the stool. The captain wore an unpleasant expression. "It wasn't a lot of money at all, captain, considering I hold what's in those boxes—my goods—in trust. Pretty nervous trust, too." I saw no harm admitting it.

"What is it you trade?" the captain slipped in.

"This and that. Whatever looks good."

"Your boxes are small."

"Lucky for me. I'd never have been able to get . . . I don't know—rattan sideboards out of B."

"No, I don't suppose . . ."

"Topher helped me very bravely, and I'm grateful to both of you," I laid it on. My body had drifted back to touch Topher's.

"Topher is brave," the captain said thoughtfully.

"Shut up," the boy breathed.

"As a matter of fact, Topher was the one who wanted desperately—" The captain abruptly censored himself when his floating gaze met mine. He began again. "What went on—well, it was a horrible thing. I won't say we're used to it here. Hardly that, but . . . Well, if you're like me—and I suspect you are—similar background, at any rate"—the comparison made me wince—"We weren't raised to live in this—this might-makes-right sort of world. We always had the rule of law, obviously, and that looks to be a pretty cozy situation, after you've been down—"

"Captain, they put animals adrift again!" Topher interrupted excitedly, but in a low, dark voice. "Look at the cow!"

I stood. A white cow floated on its back in the water. Bloated to a comic and ghastly degree, twiggy legs awry, it looked like a spectral set of bagpipes. Around it floated the corpses of other domesticated animals.

"I see. I see. Watch out, now. You have to left-rudder before long."

"What makes it fat?" the boy asked. Believe it or not, I felt a twinge, because he was asking the captain, not me.

"Some sort of gas as it rots inside—CO_2, I believe. Carbon dioxide. Maybe the scavengers where it comes from have all died. Or they know to leave it alone. Animal sensitivities are amazing sometimes."

"The fish'll eat it," I suggested.

The captain looked at me, drawing up the puffy sacs under his eyes again. I had the impression he was annoyed I may have glimpsed a secret fondness between him and his student riverboat pilot.

He continued teaching both of us in a less friendly voice. "Sometimes the villagers along here, when there's any little animal plague, will just dump the carcasses in the river. They're supposed to wait to have them examined, but they'd rather get rid of the source of infection as soon as possible. Of course, that sometimes means the problem spreads. Where are we exactly?" His arm reached behind him, rolls of fat shifting, and he tugged a legal pad from under a clutter of books and a stray mug with a dried varnish of coffee at the bottom.

"Abeam Mamajuma Island Light," Topher said. "Animals come in from the Fort Grampion river."

"They might stick in the marshy bit along Mamajuma Island. That wouldn't be so bad." He'd written a note and tore the square of paper from a corner of the sheet. One word—"animals"—I read. With a sawing motion he worked the scrap under the newly polished brass flange of a dead-seeming gauge. Or the gauge's trembling arrow measured the general vibration of the *Myrrha*. Wryly I hunted for a scrap reading, "men." "I'll report on this when we get to A." He chortled at the way that sounded. "Though I'm sure they have plenty to worry about with this—this insurrection or whatever it is. Were you in B long before it started?" he asked me.

"At the executions," I said quickly, wanting to seem well-informed. "Or so I heard. No. I came into the country a couple of weeks ago. From Z. I was only in B briefly. I was waiting for the trading companies to approve my credentials."

"Nice how the companies have taken over the business of passports and . . ." the captain muttered bitterly. "No wonder people want them thrown out. Not that the government is capable of—well, they can't even field a livestock inspector or two. Morons."

"The atmosphere was odd," I volunteered. "In B. I had a feeling, even though I was a stranger, that I was more alert to what was about to happen than the people who lived there. Not that it wasn't sudden. Someone told me it started after the executions."

"Very sudden." The captain looked ahead as if testing whether strangers really saw more clearly than natives. "They execute people all the time. Gruesome truth. Z! Z! How lucky you are! You live there?"

"Yes——"

"*Now*," the captain said to Topher. "Left-rudder to 044°. It's common practice to cross the line of the Mamajuma Island range this haul and steady on Light 18. When the B19 buoy's broad on the starboard beam, you'll be back on the range line. Then it gets a bit tricky. We'll go for one-and-three-eighths miles and look for Sammy-Oka's marina to starboard. All lit up. He has a generator. Or did. If he's even still alive. Anyway, there's the old pulp mill behind it. Tell me when we're there. We're going to right-rudder slowly 053° and get the Topopo marsh range over the stern."

"What's tricky?"

"Because we have a tendency to head reach there—cross the range line. So as soon as we get to the so-called marina, you've always got to keep your eye out for upbound ship. Not that anyone'll be headed to B. But as a general rule. Future reference. And then, also, from Light 17 to the horizontal banded nun buoy at the head of the cutoff channel the set of the current is down the south channel to the west."

The captain looked at me sourly, making me feel like an eavesdropper. Like many people with an expertise, he had no clue it was the most beautiful thing about him. At least, for me, it made him momentarily likeable. I even felt a flicker of jealousy. Navigation was something the captain and Topher shared.

The boy's hands jumped from the wheel. He dried them on his thighs before quickly regripping the lacquered wood. He threw a smile backward toward the captain and me. He noticed something. He let go of the wheel again to twist backward and stroke the captain's forearm hurriedly. A mosquito. He left a short streak of blood on skin like powdered latex. The captain didn't react at all to the service.

I was starting to feel I was lingering. If I let myself slip down to a lower level of existence, I could probably stay there forever, saying nothing and staring at the way the ruby gleam of a switch light cast a glow from below on the tensed fasces of Topher's wrists. The other two would think it strange, but I could just stay there. There'd be no way they could get through to me.

Odd, but it was now—down here—that I again noticed the captain's rings. He was turning them on his fingers like dials. He spoke, which dragged me back. "No. They execute people all the time." He sounded sincerely disgusted. "It can't have been that alone. May have happened at the same time—happened to have happened. The Mandarins—nasty bunch—just a local version of the companies, except for all the head-chopping, and, you know, in a way they're more comprehensible to the people. Oppressive, maybe—"

"But who are the people?" I broke in. "Mandarins, Karak, local company employees, Rapithwinists, Marxists in the cities? Which groups?"

The captain frowned in annoyance. "Well, all of those. Plus Topher and me. The people are at a lower level than groups. Clearly. This is far below groups. Maybe it's like an earthquake. Just something that happens at a certain point in the history of a people and nothing to do about it."

"You can't be saying there hasn't been exploitation and brutality.

Or that those things don't have to be. The country stinks of anxiety and fear and desperation."

"Listen!" Topher exclaimed. "The Recors shoal gong buoy 12."

"We're coming along, thank God," the captain murmured. His chin sank into his jowls, which folded neatly like bolts of pink silk. His hand brushed at the cobwebs of political life, and he said to me, "Undoubtedly. Undoubtedly. Oh, of course. It's a terrible place. An awful country. And in total disorder. Back there we—we saw terrible things. Of course."

"You think things like this are inevitable? Historically?"

He sighed. "I wanted to say . . ." He was changing the subject. He made himself sound businesslike. "I wanted to tell you what I planned to do with the contents of this box." He toed it lightly. At once I was wary. "As it happens, a cousin, and close friend, of my beloved friend, the late captain of this vessel, works at Anders Willis Trading Company in A. So it all comes together, in a manner of speaking . . . Did I say this already? If you're going to be in A any time at all, it might be useful for the company to speak with you about—events. Back there. At the hong. Nobody approves of it, but the companies are the power in this country, frankly, and I think they'll be the ones most interested in mounting—well, I won't say 'mounting an investigation.' But I feel sure they'll want to know whatever—whatever you may have witnessed."

I told him I'd do what he thought best.

"And if you went straight to them, you might, in a sense, head off government involvement. If you waited, eventually the government might want interviews and an investigation—all to no point, naturally—but the whole thing could become time-consuming. This way it's over and done with. If the government squawks, Anders Willis can tell them, 'We've dealt with it.'" He gave me a quick glance I didn't like.

After I left, I thought I heard him begin a quiet remark to Topher, "You see, what did I tell you . . . ?"

ON THE BED'S damp, twisted coverlet, my feet skewed over the edge and resting on boxes, I was prey to the usual fear, but also to diffuse anger, twinges of the black haughtiness that eats at you when you feel like a chump. I couldn't figure out why I felt disrespected. The captain? I didn't like this overladen creaking of events in which my part was so small and uninfluential. I was exhausted but unable to sleep. On my shut eyelids I studied the kaleidoscopic phosphenes. Those purling fireworks had obsessed me as a lonely child. Here they were again, pretty inducements to stay at the lowest level of existence, even when your eyes were shut and it was time to sleep.

Also like a child, I couldn't help hearing indistinguishable talk. Murmured conversations spiraled down into the river under the word-eating rumble of the engine and the monotonous sloshing of the floats. Now and then I could make out the tenor splash of a fish or the murky bell buoys or, when we reached A's industrial outskirts, the shouts of nightwatchmen and the mechanical bleating of docklands. Each spot struck me as the perfect place to escape with my treasure. A hellhole, maybe, like every place in this country, but so diminutive and obscure to the ear that I imagined it almost—relatively—delightful.

I understood one exchange during the night. It took place in the corridor outside my cabin. I recognized the captain by his rasping breath and shambling step. The man in the neighboring cabin must have recognized him, too. He piped up in a wakeful, cultivated voice, "Captain, is it far now? How much longer?" The question couldn't help but sound childish. There was a long, embarrassed pause. The captain would be fussy about talking through closed doors. Maybe it was the speaker's air of helplessness, or my own, but the captain's voice surprised me when it came—reassuring, gently paternal. "Five hours or so. We're making good time. Sleep well." I dreaded the morning and arrival in A.

(It's time to end this talk about no places. It's time to start telling the whole truth. From now on no more antiquated alphabetical mumbo-jumbo. Where I've written *A*, I mean the faded emporium of Alejandrina—the real, the disappointing, the ever-receding object of so many daydreams. Alejandrina.)

4

PASSENGERS AND CREW attended to each other blankly the next day. We were in a sour state. No one had had a restful night. Groggy, squinting, grumpy, standoffish. Each of us lurched through morning thoughts: the mind zooms in crazily on an idea or thing, on a memory or project, pans over other ones, while we sense in our bones, but refuse to admit, what a clunky mechanism consciousness really is, prone to chill, overheat, race, break down, slow, falter, drift and, worst of all, stop. One has to steady oneself to get through the day.

The lone, monosyllabic steward, his arm draped with a heavy napkin stained with last night's coffee, refused to meet anyone's eyes. He slouched in perfect immobility next to a table and coffee urn on the open top deck. No risk of snipers this far downriver, or not yet. Most of the passengers had gathered, but there was almost no interaction. Even Van Loon was uncommunicative. He emptied a basket of its three last buns in plastic sleeves and squatted by the railing. He was curly-haired, haggard and unshaven. A little older than me, I now saw. Last night he'd sounded younger. I kept my distance in case he revived and wanted to talk. Still uncomfortable being away from my treasure for long, I got my coffee and slipped back to the cabin.

Our collective mood made Alejandrina the perfect destination. Sometimes the tropics are as gray as November in Z but as close-feeling as a sickroom. Alejandrina was a commercial city that had never had any time for culture. It boomed as a regional shipping center, then just as suddenly it shrank. (A neighboring so-called republic, a nicely stable tyranny really, built a more modern container port.) Alejandrina teemed with styleless white eight- and ten-storey buildings, many of them empty. It was easy to get lost, though the streets were spacious. The port's row of four immense cranes, rusting monstrously, was the nearest thing to a landmark. Whole quarters of the city were dull, depopulated, mute. Wild dogs loped through empty neighborhoods at a tipsy trot that made them look poisoned or faint from starvation, both of which they often were. Their corpses were the lumps seen on gravel-strewn berms along the few busy roads.

High-smelling and in a drunken stupor, Old Ol was one of the first off the *Myrrha*. We didn't speak, but he looked at me as he passed, and he looked back at me again from the street, eyes bloodshot, face bright red except where tense creases in his forehead made for bloodless stripes of a yellowish pallor.

Arms folded identically, Topher and I watched the passengers and crew disembark. I wasn't going to unload my boxes until the crowds dispersed. A government security nabob installed at a card table on the dock was shaking down the passengers. Holding white or yellow slips of paper signed by the captain crew members waited in line impatiently at another table. Eyes hunting for bars, friends, crimps, they cooled their heels until it was their turn to be harassed by government and company officials.

The so-called Chain Locker was the sailors' gathering place, a small, dilapidated building. Ranged next to it were beat-up caddies with squared tubular handles used to move baggage and cargo around the dock. When things quieted down, I sent Topher for one of them. Since he was due to be released anyway, the captain loaned him to me with an ill-natured shrug.

In B, I'd been offered a secure location for my boxes, Bottom hong. There'd been no time to arrange for one here before escaping. I'd deliberately mentioned—to the captain, Topher, Ol and Van Loon—a hotel I said I meant to hole up in. I wrote the name of the same place on the security nabob's form, which I slid across his card table with a five-dollar wink. Except I wasn't going to stay there. I'd scouted another place on first coming into the country, when I paused in Alejandrina several days before heading upriver. It wasn't entirely secure—it was just another hotel, after all—but I figured, if no one knew where I was, if no one knew what was in my boxes, if no one knew anything about me, if no one knew anything about anything about anything at all . . . Incantatory secrecy was the only plan I could come up with.

I jumped when Van Loon appeared smirking at my elbow.

"Don't tell me you know him." It wasn't quite a smirk. More insinuating than that. He was trying to suppress it.

I had no idea what he meant. Not wanting to look befuddled, I frowned.

"The kid. The captain's kid." He nodded toward Topher, still trying to suppress his expression. An involuntary one, I realized, not meant to be a smirk or insinuating after all.

"What? Topher? He's just a deckhand."

"That's right. Topher Smith." His expression flashed clearly for a second—distaste. "You looked chummy, that's all."

I shrugged. "He's helping me. I hired him for an hour. To move stuff."

"You have cargo on board?"

"Baggage and—some things. Why're you acting like there's something funny about him?"

"Oh, no. He's harmless. Just . . . a bit of a lowlife. I couldn't figure out what the connection was. With you. You don't seem . . ."

I was too tired for this. "Why do you care? How do you know him anyway?"

"Oh, he's known." Van Loon seemed to decide he was being too mysterious. "It's really not a big deal. I was only thinking, because you're new to the country and you don't know who's who and what's what . . ." I stared at him and waited. His eyes screwed up, "Are you sure you don't know what I'm talking about?" He tried to sound cajoling, which didn't come naturally to him. He was more earnest than teasing. His boy's face, graying, sagging a bit with age and too little sleep, wasn't built for irony or deceit.

"I don't," I said. "I see a kid. He helps me with my stuff. I'm a businessman." For some reason I blushed. We were in the shadow of the *Myrrha*, out of the sun, so I hoped it wasn't obvious.

"I'm sorry. I was only trying to be friendly," he said. He sounded sincere.

"What is he? A thief? Should I be worried?"

"No, no." Van Loon obviously wrestled with a qualm now. "Listen, none of us is better than anybody else," he said virtuously. "I made a mistake, I guess. I'm exhausted, completely done in, after . . ." He squinted upriver toward B. "Sorry. You promised me a drink, right? So we can talk about what happened at the hong."

I nodded.

"I'm going to hold you to it." He smiled, to all appearances the nicest guy in the world.

LOADED UP, THE CADDY, basically a steel platform on wheels, was hard to manage. I wondered if it hadn't been a mistake waiting till the crowds cleared. The handfuls of loiterers looked threatening. The dull sky had turned stormy. It was early afternoon and neither Topher nor I had eaten. The cart kept getting stuck on the cobbled dock. More and more exasperated, Topher rocked it violently, until it lurched a foot or so then stuck in another gap between paving stones. I kept shoving the boxes back into place on the platform. If one were to fall and break open . . . The going was easier once we got to the macadamized roadway of the main waterfront street, King Alfred's Way. But the castered wheels still weathervaned unpredictably, so we moved in zigzags.

A knot of soldiers strolled casually enough, but why were they patrolling here? News about B may have spread already. I wasn't the only one feeling anxious. Anxiety seemed generalized. People suddenly looked at the sky or at buildings, noticing things apparently, though I never noticed anything myself. It was almost irritating. What were they looking at? The wind reminded me of the weather yesterday in B. The gusts seemed to shuffle nervousness from person to person. I'd hoped to dismiss Topher, but there was no way I could handle the caddy by myself. So he, at least, was going to know which hotel I was really staying at. This tiny breach of secrecy felt like a disaster. I knew I was overwrought, but wheeling my treasure around an unfamiliar city without any guards or any serious protection at all—the plan now struck me as insane. I was more naive than Mr. Haver.

King Alfred's Way turned, running up a slight incline away from the water toward the old city center and my hotel. Topher and I both had to push the cart along this stretch. We'd gone a hundred yards or so when, shoulder to the cart, I turned back and glimpsed a man jogging our way. He wore a green jumpsuit like a mechanic's uniform. I didn't like the situation. He was rounding the corner from the dock and might well be coming after us. Up ahead, I spotted some kids running. Also suspicious. It was maddening. I couldn't keep my eye on everyone, look up and down the street at the same time. An almost involuntary sound came out of me, something between a groan and "OK, I . . ." I stopped pushing and straightened, folding my arms in a show of stubbornness.

"Topher . . ."

He saw I was looking at the man in a green jumpsuit. With a grin he started to answer me, "Oh! Hey—" He fell to his knees.

I'd heard a small thud, which made me look wildly at the boxes. After a second's delay, Topher let out a tremendous howl of pain that bled into a string of bitter curses. The man in the jumpsuit stopped, then started up again, faster. He was definitely coming toward us. Other passersby heard the scream. They looked ready to come over, too.

When Topher lost his grip on the caddy's handle, it shifted slightly. My fingers splayed over the boxes. I propped my ankle against the downslope side of the cart. Still on his knees, holding his head, Topher shouted rhythmically, more in anger at this point. He got up sluggishly, like somebody climbing out of a mud bath.

The group of kids had dodged off in a different direction, running much faster now, which looked like guilt. They slipped through a huge mauve-painted door. It closed behind them. I didn't realize Topher had even spotted these boys, but when he finally lifted his face to me, teary and enraged, he spat out, "Where the fuck did they go?"

Woodenly, I pointed to the mauve door. Topher staggered to a trot and was soon at the door, pounding on it and making it tremble. A passerby, with dainty malice or righteousness, pressed a silver button next to the door. The lock buzzed. Topher swung the door in and blundered into a dim courtyard.

The man in the green jumpsuit was next to me now. "What are you doing?" he screamed accusingly, his neck inflated like a bullfrog's, venous and blotched red. He was a friend apparently. It was reasonable enough. He thought I should be helping Topher and wouldn't know that I could never abandon the boxes. Still, there was something unpleasant about him. He was freckled,

thick-lashed, small and small-featured. It wasn't just his rage at
that moment. I could tell, even at his best, he would be a humor-
less, suspicious, hot-headed person. He seemed prepared to stay
and argue with me.

"Go help him," I said quietly.

He raised his hands and scrabbled at the air in front of my face
as if to shred my composure, such a strange gesture that one of
the people around us began to laugh.

The man in the jumpsuit ran after Topher, nearly spraining his
ankle on the new-potato-sized rock that had just struck Topher's
head and fallen to the street. When he got to the mauve door,
he swung it open so violently it hit an inner wall with an oaken
boom. Looking down at the rock, I winced. That little thud had
sounded like wood, too.

I thought the group of strangers around me would relax now,
smile, want to chat with each other about the drama, ask what
it had been all about, where was I from and, by the by, what
might I have in my boxes. I was ready to be cool, rude even, to
drive them away. But there was no amused tut-tutting or friendly
commentary about an unfortunate event which fortunately didn't
involve—ahem—oneself. Instead, the faces around me returned
to ticcy sullenness. It wasn't normal. Could they have been hoping for worse? When they realized nothing more was going to
happen, they drifted off with a few grudging nods at most. I was
left alone as I wanted to be, but it wasn't reassuring. It didn't feel
good at all standing there in the open with my treasure.

I had to swallow a weird flicker of petulance when, after a long time, Topher and the man in the jumpsuit reappeared through the mauve door shaking their heads in failure.

Topher touched his temple and swore. The man came up to me and demanded, "Who are you?"

I didn't bother answering him. I was looking at Topher with concern. The man in the jumpsuit followed my gaze and said, "Oh, Jesus, Topher. Man. You got to get yourself cleaned up." He pointed a little squeamishly at Topher's shoulder where the blood had spattered his shirt.

Topher waved his hand. The wound wasn't painful unless he touched it. But when he looked sidelong down at his shoulder, he commented absently, "Shit, I'm really bleeding."

The man dug a paper towel from his pocket and made a move to blot the wound, then just handed the wad of dirty paper to Topher.

"I got to talk to him a sec," Topher explained to me apologetically. Eyeing me from under his gingerly dabbing hand he appeared coy. Neither of them bothered with an introduction. They moved a few steps away and spoke in low voices. I couldn't figure out their connection. They definitely weren't related. The man in the jumpsuit was older, my age. He was smaller than Topher, runtish even, but scrappy, with little hands and monkey-like bowed legs. I watched him squeeze his eyes closed in a whiney sort of expression when Topher whispered something he didn't like.

Topher retreated in my direction. Their conversation came up to full volume.

" . . . I got to go back to work," the man in the jumpsuit was saying. "Maybe somebody heard something on the radio at Anders Willis."

Topher shrugged—a little encouragingly, all the same.

"Who is this guy?" the man asked him.

Topher looked at me, but still I didn't answer. Instead, I said, "Let me look at that a second." I took the boy's cheeks between my hands and straightened his face on mine. "I'll be careful," I said, because he was about to flinch. I didn't touch the wound. The other two were impressed. I looked like I knew what I was doing. The wound still wept, and a thread of blood ran along my forefinger to the web of my thumb. The blood moved so slowly I got chills. The creeping fluid must have tickled Topher, too. Under my palms I felt the warm, gorgeous sensation of a tremor.

I remembered from my time as a camp counselor that a sneaking concussion could be spotted in the pupils, I couldn't remember how. Maybe their dilation was affected. With an almost ceremonious gentleness I covered Topher's eyes. While I waited a minute, I dropped my gaze to the boxes (secure), scanned a few strangers still on the street, the darkening sky, and looked, finally, at the man in the jumpsuit, whose face registered hostility. When I took my hand from Topher's eyes, the two oil-black pupils shrank suddenly, hesitated and rebounded a bit. They floated on glistening, shattered aquamarine starbursts. "It looks all right," I said. "Why don't you go back, though? Rest and get something to eat."

"What'll you do?"

"He'll help, I guess, or he can send me somebody."

"No, no," Topher sounded irritated. "No!" he repeated, when the other muttered that I'd have to pay.

"Go!" the man urged. "I'm sure he can afford it."

Topher insisted. "No. I'll go. I know the hotel."

"This guy just came in with you? He was on the *Myrrha*?" I stared at the man long or hard enough to prompt a belligerent "What?" Then he had the balls to pitch me. "Listen, if you just came in, you wanna change some money? I got a better rate than anybody around here." His spiel was half automatic, half indifferent. A wad of the local currency was out of his pocket—little bills, filthy and limp, as always. People sometimes washed the bills in soap and water, but they were never clean.

I had to smile. "I was going to use, uh, silver," I said. I jingled the coins and knife in my pocket, in case they thought I had silver anywhere else.

The man in the jumpsuit tipped his head and repeated, "Silver," as if it were a doubtful or dangerous currency.

"Silver's fine," Topher rolled his eyes.

"Go back to the boat, Topher," the man said.

"This doesn't even hurt. No, I'm going with him."

"Why would you want to come to this city at all?" the man demanded of me, unpleasantly again. When I didn't answer, he shrugged and said to Topher, "I'm going. You manage for yourself. But take care of that . . ." He tapped his forehead. "And call me if you find out anything about—what we talked about."

"You'll find out before me. If you talk to them over there. You let *me* know."

When the man was out of earshot, Topher sighed. "Sorry," he

said. He screwed one eye tightly shut and explained, "He's sort of got a thing for me, if you know what I mean . . ." He smiled sheepishly.

"No." Under my breath I added, "I think he's a prick."

"I mean . . ." His hand started tipping back and forth. "Love. Crush. Semi-obsession. Love, I guess. It's a pain in the ass." He panted out a little unsure laughter.

"Love? Is that what this was about?"

He wiped his smile away. "No, this time was about something else. I can't explain. The love thing just makes him hard to deal with. Impossible to get through to, you know? He's either staring at me or he flies off the handle. He's not really a prick, though. More pathetic. I don't know where he gets the idea I would . . . What can I say? Poor slob doesn't have enough money." Topher waited an instant, then grinned and barked at this knee-slapper. It did seem ludicrous to imagine scuffed, rough-around-the-edges Topher could be a preening hustler or a gold digger. But if there were any truth in it, his good humor made all his wiles forgivable—whether you wanted them to be or not.

I DIDN'T LOVE the room, but I'd been here before and knew it was the particular room in the particular hotel I needed, the Colebart. The caddy and boxes took up half the space. We'd had to unload and reload to get up the single pediment step but the caddy fit, barely, in the cage of the hotel's groaning elevator. I pushed the button and we ran up the helical stair to meet it on the sixth floor. The clerk wasn't happy about this eccentricity. He

wanted my things in a storeroom or the safe. When he said he had
to know what I was taking up, I told him clocks, I was a dealer in
clocks. I wheedled, bribed him. He backed down. "The rooms .
. ." he explained vaguely in apology, as if I could have been trans-
porting something merely dirty. I decided not to fuss about his
keeping my passport, the common practice here, though I felt a
pang when he deftly chucked it into the mailbox. The more cha-
otic things got, the more people loved papers. I didn't like to be
without them. But the clerk was nice enough to fetch a bottle of
hydrogen peroxide, when I explained that my "employee" had—
obviously—had an accident. He made a small flourish, ushering
bloody Topher after me. I think there was irony in the gesture.

Topher sat on the bed looking exhausted and hot. Mechanically,
he ate a mummified cheese sandwich from a fly-specked machine
in the lobby. As he chewed, the crust of blood rippled over a
lumpy cheek. He unshuttered and threw open the French windows for air. When I held out my hand, he stopped eating again,
peeled off his shirt and handed it to me.

"Hot or cold for blood?" I wondered aloud, crumpling the shirt
into a tiny sink. It shuddered, because the caulk had lost its grip
on the wall. This wasn't a fancy hotel. "Cold, I think," I decided.

"Cold," Topher echoed with his mouth full. I think he knew.

"If you've got to go back soon, you can take one of my shirts
and get this one later. You stay on the *Myrrha*, right? Will the captain wonder where you are?"

"He'll be with the harbormaster for hours. Filing papers. It's
stupid, but . . ."

"So, who was that guy? The guy who's in love with you."

"Bill? Bill Sawtell."

He didn't say anything more, and I didn't want to press him right off. When Topher was done with the sandwich I had him stand in the light of the window, though the sky was beetling now. I took some rough paper towels from a stack on a cracked glass shelf over the sink. Dousing one with hydrogen peroxide, I dealt with his wound. It looked almost like a chip in marble because of Topher's extreme pallor, though after only a day in the sun, his shoulders, forehead and broad nose already had the flush of a burn. Next to the wound's divot a bloodless flap of skin had curled up. I tore it off. He made a somnolent noise of pain in his chest. "Sorry." I threw the tiny relic of him out the window without thinking. At the center of the pink divot were numerous red points, no longer bleeding. Pink foam rose when I dabbed the wound with hydrogen peroxide. I heard a faint sound like Cricket's warehouses going up in flames.

"But who is he?"

"Just this guy I know."

"Did I hear him say he works for Anders Willis?"

"Yeah. At some warehouse," he admitted lightly.

"That's not the captain's cousin, is it? Or it was 'cousin of my dear friend, the former captain.'"

Topher smiled. "No." He smiled harder, imagining Bill Sawtell working in the front office, I think. "Actually, he may have put in a word for them. The cousin did. When Bill and his brother needed jobs. I don't know if Anders Willis is going to stay. You think the companies'll stay in the country now?" I shrugged. Then I confessed, "No."

"You?"

"I'm going the way I came. As soon as possible. I'm going out on the *Clay*. I don't know if I'll have time for the captain's— investigation, or whatever it was."

"Mm." He stretched. "Too bad. You were the best job I had in a long time." He looked at me and dared to tease, very tentatively. "Easy mark. Big spender."

"Actually, most of this blood did come out," I throttled his shirt dry, snapped it flat and draped it over the rusted filigree rail of the window's false balcony. "Oh, and remember what I said about not wanting anybody to know my address. I'm funny about that. Keep it to yourself."

"Yeah. Too bad," he sighed. He looked out the window. "You know, you have a problem. With the *Clay*. There's no *Clay*."

"What are you talking about?"

"There's no *Clay*. It sailed."

"How do you know?"

"They post the sailing schedule outside the door of the Chain Locker." He lightly kicked the steel caddy. "I read it. *Clay* already sailed."

"Don't kick my shit," I said out of pure annoyance, not at him. "Anybody else going out?"

"Not for a while."

"Are you sure? You read the whole thing?"

"Check it out yourself."

"Damn."

"Can I ask something? Why don't you want anybody to know anything about you? Because of the money?"

"What do you mean?"

"The money, the money!" Lightly he kicked the platform cart again. "Sorry," he whispered naughtily. "What do you think, I can't hear?"

It was true. When the boxes were moved, they made a characteristic clucking, even with the padding of oakum I'd stuffed inside.

"And how much they weigh. And just the way you act. You don't want me to say anything about the money, either, I guess."

I shrugged. "I'm private, that's all. I'm an agent. It's not mine."

"Supercargo?"

"Sort of."

Now he shrugged, dissimulating, I think, enormous pleasure because I'd trusted him that far.

"Why'd your friend go down to the dock to meet the *Myrrha*? That's what happened, right? He was late and came running after us—you?"

"Who, Bill? I don't know," he lied.

"Love? Had to see you. Or you said it wasn't love. Something else."

"Could've been." He examined his wound in a spotted mirror. A finger delicately caught a last trickle of pink foam.

"You know somebody named Van Loon?"

"No."

"He warned me you're a lowlife."

"Fuck him, then."

The shutters revolved in and tapped the walls of the room.

The temperature had dropped a few degrees, and the luminous green-gray pall of the coming afternoon storm cast its light into the room. This light didn't belong to any proper hour at all, but to time perpendicular to the usual timeline, the way this country was perpendicular to the world. There was a far-off shout that could have been happiness, then a fiery crepitation of rain swelled. In an instant it was pouring. The rain was windless, but pressure drove a damp breeze through the window. Topher came over and stood in it. After a while he luxuriantly stroked the dew from his chest.

"Feels good." He grinned.

"What happened to you? I've never seen anybody with that many scars. And how come you were so pale?"

"I was in the hospital. Just got out."

Rain in the tropics sometimes falls so heavily it doesn't form drops. Topher turned and, in the tricky light, seemed to glow against a background of measureless, rustling filaments of water. I felt a deep unease that he was dangerous, the kind of unease that isn't related to real fear or real danger.

"They said I almost died." Like his spectral body, Topher's voice stood out against the din of the rain. "This was the only really bad one." He traced the scar down the middle of his chest.

"Looks like an operation scar."

"Right. They had to operate, cause my dad shot me. That was three years ago."

"You must've been a kid. Anyway, a little young to get shot up. Your dad sounds scary."

"It was an accident. And yeah, I was younger. I think I look old for my age, though, huh?"

"I don't know."

"Sixteen."

"No, then."

He chuckled as if he thought I were being harsh as a kind of joke. But I wasn't joking or being harsh at all. I was just telling him what I thought.

There was a big pavilion down by the dock, where they sometimes held dances. Colored lights and speakers were strung up under the eaves. After a few staticky sneezes, these speakers started in on some music, just audible up here through the rain, especially the thumping bass. Maybe they were testing the system. Topher immediately snapped into a spent boxer's stance, pumping his hips forward and back, dancing with a silly grin. "I'm good, no?" he demanded. He finished with a tight spin when the music abruptly died.

"Why don't you tell me about Bill Sawtell. What's the story with him?"

"Nothing. It's complicated," he groused. "It's private!" he added with a note of triumph.

"Yeah, and I *told* you my private business. So tell."

"This isn't *my* private thing. It's his. If you care, it won't matter in a day or so."

"Does it have to do with what happened at Bottom hong?"

I saw that it did. Topher didn't say anything. He closed his eyes and tried to remember the music. Forcing himself into a trance, he recapitulated the dance, hardly moving. I put my hand on his shoulder and left it there. I can't describe the effect. The dance drained out of him. He opened his eyes, but all other movement—all thought, maybe—stopped, everything except his breathing. As if he'd become a zombie—but from good not evil influence. "You must be exhausted," I said, though I didn't really think that was it. "We saw terrible things. If you want, you can sleep here. I'll go downstairs, get something to eat."

Before I was finished speaking, he childishly answered "No" about being exhausted. Then, defiantly, he whispered, "That wasn't so bad."

"Oh, yeah? The guy they strung up at Cricket hong?"

"That was bad," he admitted in a monotone.

I realized the hint of living death that had come over him had nothing to do with what we'd experienced in B. It had to do with my hand on his shoulder. My hand drained all the energy from him, but in a way he liked, or feared he liked. Even when I finally took it away, he didn't snap back to the regular level of existence. He shuffled away, eyes lowered, affectless, but suppressing, I think, nervous pleasure. He sat on the bed as if he were waiting on me. He glanced up at me. The zombie-like obedience dissipated slowly, and he said, "I am tired." Then, "And that *was* a big deal. What happened up at Bottom. I'll tell you later."

"If you won't tell me what Sawtell wanted, then tell me who's throwing rocks at you on the street? Does it have something to do with what Van Loon told me about you being known around here?"

He brightened, "This guy said I was 'known'?"

"Yeah, but not in a good way."

He shrugged. "Those were some kids I used to see. Bunch of *franquista* skinhead fags."

I almost smiled. That was a group Van Loon wasn't up on. "*Franquista?*"

"You know, fascist. Hang around with this Congolese guy who came in and opened a strip club. Except he calls it 'Society dez Ambiancers eh dez Persons Elegant.'"

Societé des Ambianceurs et des Personnes Elegantes. It was an African social club. I didn't know what they could be doing here. "Fascists? Are you saying this was political?"

He laughed at me. "Political types and, like, Rapithwinists *kill* people. They don't throw rocks." He laughed helplessly. He was pushing it, trying to needle me. "You thought that was serious! No. Man, that was just about a jacket. I used to be friends with this kid. He grew up as a Seventh Day Adventist, totally fucked up, which made him sort of psycho when he started at the strip club. It wasn't love or anything, but we were friends. We traded jackets. And now he hates me. We couldn't stay friends, because we argued about religion all the time. He wants his jacket back, but it's too big a deal now."

"Those kids were friends of yours?"

"Former. Used to be. I don't know. Maybe a couple of them still are." All at once he was melancholy. "It was too bad that happened. I hate it when people go away. You know, even in the sense of just not being there for you." For the first time since that night I hired him in B, a trace of the maudlin glub-glub got into his voice. "I always try to be there for my friends. I would never abandon people. But it's happened to me a lot, you know? Some guy I thought 'This is great' and then the next day he's gone, or he acts like he never knew you."

I was anxious for him. It didn't seem safe or wise to be readily confessional like this. I said something I thought he'd find ridiculous. "Was this some kind of a gang you were in?"

He did laugh. He shook his head. "Shit. A gang. A gang!" He was cheery again. He rubbed his stomach. "I'm glad I ate something." With busy, kid-like energy he went to the window and said, "You know, I've never been in a hotel room before." The rain was slackening.

"Topher . . ." I said, putting my hand on his shoulder again. But I had nothing to say to him. I only said his name as a natural-sounding feint, so I could put my hand on him. Again, I left it there. But I was concentrating this time. Again, he sank to the lowest level of existence. Merely breathing. The effect was like magic. It was the reason I had to try it a second time. At my touch docility suffused a rambunctious kid. I could easily see myself becoming obsessed with the power. I went a little further. I turned him to face me. He turned as easily as the window shutters. Gently I pushed him a step or two backward. I was frowning intently, as if I were a scientist, and this was the experiment my career depended on.

I was at a low level of existence myself. I knew I was a decent guy, but my decency could stretch to include whatever I happened to do or want to do. The really bad thing was always a little farther along, nothing I was aiming at. In this case, the bad thing might have been a cruelty of timing I refused to pay any attention to. My plan to leave Alejandrina and his complaint "the next day he's gone" were the same thing. I know it sounds vain, but the kid was fascinated by me.

I slipped below the level of existence where I knew anything I did could cause future pain. I ran my hand over his chest, frowning even harder. The boyish nipples, which had been as flat as scars, dragged under my palm like tiny upholstered buttons. Whatever material he was made of was the most luxurious stuff I'd ever touched, but it was stretched across stone. It was strange to have so much power over someone who completely lacked softness. As if it were a very ordinary thing to act out my passions, I got on my knees dragging my cheek along his body until my ear was pressed to his thigh. When I closed my eyes to concentrate on his thigh's warmth through the cool of the pant leg glazed by rain, I think, a long way off, some unrecognized emotion flickered. But I'm not sure. I'm a disciplined man. Though nothing but my own tough-ness prompted me, I stood up, smiled, clapped his shoulder, got him a shirt and sent him back to the *Myrrha*. When he asked in a monotone if we'd see each other again, I said, "Of course."

THAT NIGHT I regretted my laxness with the treasure. I couldn't decide exactly what I'd done that was lax, but I blamed myself anyway. Maybe for carting the boxes through the streets unpro-tected, or secreting them here in a hotel room with a contempt-ible lock on the door and a duplicate key downstairs. But where else could I have taken them? I didn't trust anyone in Alejandrina. I had a premonition things were going to fall apart. I wanted my treasure at hand, and I didn't want anyone else's hands anywhere near it. The last time I'd had a feeling things were turning bad was in B and I'd been right.

Topher and the day clerk knew where my boxes were. The day

clerk probably told the hotelier, and by now the night clerk and the rest of the staff might know. Topher also knew what was inside the boxes. That meant, despite his promise, I should count on the captain, Sawtell and the odd impoverished friend knowing, too. It seemed lax of me.

A grandiose colonial relic, the Colebart was one of the oldest buildings in Alejandrina. Some rooms, like mine, were cubicles chopped out of bigger rooms. Many were taller than they were long or wide. The cubicles opened on to vast, dim halls whose original moss-colored marble floors were a wreck. There were long stretches of bare concrete with irregular patches of bathroom mosaic, old repairs that had buckled and cracked. Plumbing and electricity had come a generation after the place was built. The painted or insulation-bandaged arteries were visible everywhere, driving through moldings and cement block walls and floorboards. While all the rooms had sinks, each floor shared showers and toilets. On the floor I chose, the sixth, there'd been some kind of tearoom or morning room, eight windows wide, looking toward the front of the hotel. I'd figured it out when I was first given this room.

On the high ceiling over my bed was an acanthus something-or-other, a couple of lolling, satanic tongues heavily draped with cobwebs. On the ceiling of one of the toilet stalls down the hall matching plasterwork ran through a cheaply built wall as if to join up with the acanthus leaves in my room. A fragment of marble— piss-stained or just yellow, I couldn't tell—was under the commode. Between the toilets and my room, more marble fragments and more acanthus leaves decorated another room. This was the

sixth-floor shower room. Strangely, it was enormous. Six windows were blacked out by the exterior signs reading:

COLEBART HOTEL

There were three showers, all open, Italian-style. The windows
let in no sun, and there was only a single weak bulb, in the corner over the showers, to light the entire space, which, I began to
understand, had been some kind of tearoom where the forefa-
thers had spackled toast with marmalade and chatted mahogany.

My first night in the country I was kept up for hours by backpack-
ing pals having sex in the shower. Instead of complaining about the
room, the next day I tried to figure out how I could hear them so
clearly. In the shower room, next to the showers I found what looked
like a portholed kitchen door. The porthole had been replaced by
plywood. The door opened on to a kind of closet in the wall. After a
little study I realized three dumbwaiters had been combined, floored
over and made into a closet, a closet which had originally served
my room on the other side. I could reach in and knock the back of
the bowed, wallpapered sheet of Masonite that was all that sepa-
rated my room from its former closet. The dead space and Masonite
acted as an eardrum for shower sex. On this side, the shower room
side, a padlock latch had been installed for security, but since access
to my room had been sealed off by the Masonite, it didn't need to
be locked anymore. The closet wasn't being used. The maids kept
their columns of cheap toilet paper and tubs of mini-soaps in junked
armoires by the windows. The closet held only a large cardboard
box, mildewed and decaying, and a gray steel set of office shelves,
empty. I was going to hide my boxes there.

People were still up and about at two AM. I slept and forced myself to get up at three. Even at three, I wanted to be cautious, so I patrolled the floors below mine before starting. I went barefoot and used the immense, shallow-stepped staircase instead of the noisy elevator squeezed into its turnings. The place was dead. I could hear the buzzing of streetlights outside. Wandering around the dark hotel gave me a childlike sense of disobedience, but I quashed it. Nighttime thoughts of Rasmussen and Hale shamed me.

I slid home the bolt on the shower room door. I hadn't needed to examine the steel shelves last time. Now I did so carefully. If the shelves were deep enough, I could get all twenty-four boxes in. I used my forearm to measure. My intimacy with the boxes was such that I knew not only their actual dimensions—9" x 5" x 16½"—but their dimensions relative to my body—inner elbow half-bent to farthest crease of wrist x tip of middle finger to "heart line" x tip of middle finger to outer elbow. The shelves were only twelve inches deep and the closet didn't have any spare depth. I must have spent fifteen minutes caressing, embracing the steel shelves with my hands and forearms—calculating.

The extraordinary weight of the boxes was another consideration. The shelves were only reinforced by the folds of metal at their edges. I figured all but two would fit. I meant to load four boxes on to each of the five main shelves and two on the narrower top shelf. I debated stacking the two extra boxes on the topmost pair, but it would be almost impossible to lift them that high. Understand, each box weighed something over eighty-three pounds, that is, a touch less than half my own weight. I opened the cardboard box and found it a quarter full of buttons, many brass-plated with a bold *C* (for Colebart) in relief. I decided I could fit the two extra boxes on top of the buttons.

Even though I had to carry each box out of my room (using the cart would have been too noisy), lug it down the hall, set it on the shower room floor, bolt the door, heave the box into place and then go back, no insomniac surprised me and I was able to get the job done in almost perfect silence. Once, when I put the fourth box on the second shelf, the metal buckled slightly and let out a gong-like ringing, surprisingly loud. I was petrified. Nobody stirred. On the third, fourth and fifth shelves, in an agony of muscle control, I had to let the weight of the boxes pass from me to the shelf as slowly as a rose opens. The buckling sound, when it came, was a muted gulp, steel swallowing silver.

In the course of my twenty-four trips, all of yesterday's bruises were refreshed. And I couldn't help worrying, the way I had at the hong, that my plan was a little off or out-of-true or crazy. My overriding concern, more psychological than logical maybe, was that I, and only I, know the location of my treasure. The hotel's storage room might be more secure, but it wasn't secret.

Just before closing the portholed door, I did something I'd sworn I would never do. I was running low on cash, so I took an advance. Maybe it was tension, exhaustion, the need to hurry . . . I did it without letting myself think. I opened the last box and took out ten, then twelve, silver dollars. I scratched the blue lid with one of the coins, so I'd know which box had 1,488 coins instead of 1,500.

I had one last thing to do before I could sleep. I had to remove the Masonite access panel on my side of the closet and secure the portholed door from the inside with a rope tied around its inner handle. For this I needed a screwdriver and rope. I don't mean to brag about my foresight. In fact, even I find something off-putting, nearly tragic, about my gift for obsessive planning—a human being should be preoccupied by something else—I never knew what. Anyway, although this whole plan was conceived in the middle of yesterday's panic in B, I'd had the presence of mind to steal a length of rope and two screwdrivers, Phillips and standard, from the hong. The Phillips wasn't a perfect fit, but it worked. I was finished and asleep by five when the shower pipes started clanging.

I dreamt I was hurrying over endless, luminous putting green hills. The sky was green-gray. All over the vast lawns, as regularly as tulips in rows and as far as the eye could see, silver coins were spinning. None ever fell. The ones I toppled or scattered as I ran rearranged themselves and popped back to their edges and started spinning again. Far ahead, Dadi Anton, carrying the naked, sheet-white body of an adolescent, leapt on and on through the hills with unreal energy. I was falling behind.

5

WHAT HAD HAPPENED in B affected the captain more deeply than he let on, even to himself. (Follow along now. Don't ask me how I know all this.) After his endless meeting with the harbormaster, he scrubbed false joviality from his mind. In his private cabin he sat on his extra-wide box bed and drank more than usual. He was an invisible drunk, unlike the spectacularly red and teetering Ol, who, at that same moment, slipped from a wooden wharf edge rubbed soft as jute and fell through a clutter of flotsam into the oily, clucking water of Alejandrina's harbor.

The captain buried his nose in praying hands. He scratched his mosquito bite with the face of his diamond ring. He soon reached a plateau of incomplete drunkenness, unable to go further. In his gloom, death seemed close. Not an unrealistic fear in light of his

obesity and alcoholism, the climate, and his near-constant pul-
monary trouble. He knew it and often mourned for himself in
advance. But as close as death seemed, sleep, which he knew had
to be even closer—he was exhausted—felt inaccessible. Nerves
and alcohol had combined in a fatigued, provisional, all but useless
sort of alertness. In self-disgust he got up, letting his weight settle
on archless, swollen feet. He'd shuffle out for air, he told himself.
Actually, he was going to see whether Topher had returned.

He felt a need to act out his woe, if only in a small or absurd
way, so he let his body slump tragically against the bulkhead. As he
staggered forward parts of his belly, thigh and upper arm dragged
along the wall in the manner of a snail's foot.

TOPHER LIVED ON the *Myrrha*, but he had no fixed sleeping
place. He might take an empty cabin or curl up on a woven Karak
mat in the pilothouse. He sometimes pretended to be a hunted
man, choosing a different spot night after night, because he'd
heard of an anti-government terrorist leader who never slept in
the same place twice for security's sake. Tonight he slept on one of
the unused cots in the strong room. It was stifling, so he stripped
to his underwear and dragged everything off the cot but one over-
bleached sheet. He was asleep almost instantly. Several flies strut-
ted confidently over his scars and the near-invisible down at his
temple and at the base of his spine.

Less than an hour later, the tickling of the flies woke him, and
he couldn't fall back to sleep. He was wired. It was probably on
account of what had happened in B, but he couldn't put his finger

on it. He rolled onto his back. An almost painfully rigid erection had nuzzled past the waistband of his underwear. It wasn't sexual in the least, but he stroked it idly like an importunate pet and yawned and debated doing something about it. The rigidity felt like the unpleasant kind that might not go away, even if he went to the trouble of beating off. Which would be the fifth time since that afternoon, so he didn't.

He scanned the untouched cots and one that was torn apart and stinking. He wondered how the men in the hong had gotten word to the captain about their insane plan to stay behind. Then his mind wandered to something I'd said, which had wounded him. My too harsh question about how he came by so many scars. Though he had a precious kernel of self-love, in that depressing room and at that dark hour, he let himself get upset thinking about his body's damage. It had happened, he reflected, because he'd never had anyone to take care of him. The thought was sad rather than bitter.

His frustrated sleeplessness took a shadowy turn. He dreaded everyone he loved would die. His former friends would be exterminated when the fighting came. Sawtell would expire from a freak heart attack after learning what had happened in B. The captain would suffocate under the weight of his own fat. And even I—I would be murdered for my money by Rapithwinists or government agents.

He thought about me. My poise—without, apparently, a friend in the world—was a mystery to Topher. It fascinated and alarmed him. My privacy looked like a terrifying wilderness, and he couldn't figure out why anyone would want to wander around there forever. He decided I was the most formidable person he'd met in his whole life till then. If I was slightly crazy, he also allowed I wasn't actually dangerous.

TOPHER HEARD THE CAPTAIN wheezing and buttons sliding along the bulkhead outside the strong room door. He flipped onto his stomach and pretended to sleep. Even the pretense was surprisingly gratifying.

Delighted to have found the boy, the captain made a drunkard's elaborate, noisy effort to be silent. He couldn't sit just anywhere. He had to search and calculate, as anyone does who carries so much weight, as I had to do with my boxes. If he sat in the middle of one of the cots, the rail would give out. So with great care he sat toward the head of one, where the metal tubing was flush with and braced against the bulkhead. He perched his weight on the rail gingerly. Too far back and the steel net under the thin mattress might break. Even so, the rail squealed.

He clasped his hands over laps of his belly and contemplated the beautiful boy dolorously. Since he'd shown the sleeper such elephantine courtesy, he thought he was probably due for a little attention himself. He cleared his throat. This midnight visit had many precedents. Topher waited until the captain actually spoke.

"You awake, Tophe?"

Topher groaned, got up on his elbows, fluttered his eyes open—none of it very convincing. It didn't matter. This time he was actually glad for company. "Oh, captain. Not feeling good?"

"No, no. I feel OK." The captain manufactured a pitifully unhealthy inhalation, though.

"Sound tired."

"Tired? Yes."

"Need something?"

The captain's voice skewed from a whimper to an authoritative basso. "You take your last pills? Your antibiotics?"

"Yup." Topher wiggled his thumb against the sheet. "All better." Now that he could do it without flaunting a hard-on, he turned onto his side, resting his cheek on the heel of his palm. Wincing slightly, he dug his hand into his underwear and diddled his balls so they hung comfortably.

"Your balls OK?" the captain demanded in the same daddy-like tone of voice.

"Yeah, yeah." Topher waved him off. One of Topher's medical emergencies had been the time the cords of his testicles knotted up causing an extremely painful inflammation and swelling. The doctor figured it had happened after the kid wore a too-small jockstrap during a stint dancing on a painted plywood cube for money that hadn't been as easy-come as hoped for.

"You cause me so much worry!" the captain veered back to mewling. "Aye-yi-yi!" he exclaimed. "Look what you've done to your head! Oh, Topher! I won't even ask what it was," he said pitifully. "I just hope he paid you well enough, your Mr. Rich Supercargo."

"Mmm."

"I wager it's money he's got in those boxes. Shape and weight. Unmistakable, really."

Topher shrugged, keeping a loyal silence.

"Wouldn't be at all surprised if he had part of Anders Willis's treasure there. The gold." The captain was insinuating something he didn't believe but wished to spread around.

"Did you get any?" Topher was talking about the single Anders Willis box that the captain had opened in private.

"Topher!" the captain whispered, affronted. "No, I only wonder about the gold because of the way he was acting in B. So anxious to get away."

"He said you were the one who was anxious. And you were. And anyway how did you know those guys were going to stay behind at the hong?" When it was plain the *Myrrha* was ready to leave, Topher had offered to run inside to get the men, but the captain told him he'd gotten word they felt secure enough and were planning to stay behind.

"Well, that's just it, Topher. It was him. He was the one in the hong, the one who'd spent time with them. He assured me."

"He did? Stoker told me Old Ol told him there wasn't any plan to stay behind."

"Ol was so drunk. But then, who really knows? I had to—to make a decision based on the information I was given. By your Mr. Rich . . . "

"Why do you say he's rich?"

"Oh, these things are obvious. Air of entitlement, greed, sucking the—the energy and life from everyone around him, mannered . . . I know the type—the yachting type . . ." Making a great molten expression of sorrow, the captain moaned. "Oh, Topher I know why you think I might want to hijack some of Anders Willis's gold, but I didn't. There wasn't anything but what I said in that box. It's the rich ones who steal. They can't even *have* without it being exactly the same as stealing. They're so cold! I wish I was brave enough to steal gold for you. But I'm not. I'm weak. And it's just because I don't have two coins to rub together that I've decided I'll have to sell the *Myrrha*." This was a familiar theme. "Pennies on the dollar with the way things are. Then I'll be dead soon. You'll get the proceeds, of course."

"I want the boat," Topher said. "And I don't want you to die."

"But if I die on the boat, no one will be able to get me off to bury me. They'll have to scuttle her with me on board. How'd you like that? Then you'd have nothing!"

"Captain . . ." Topher said gently.

"No, I simply have to sell her. No one'll be going to B for a long time. What's the point? If we leave her here, she'll be requisitioned. Or if the insurrectionists stir things up, they might burn her! And even if by some miracle things settle down, you'd never get a license to operate. Neither of us has the money to bribe the morons who run things in this country."

"Things change. I see you living a long time."

"*Haruspex, Magus, Chaldaeus, Vaticinator!*"

"What's that mean?"

"It means you're a false prophet. You're wrong. I'm dying."

"You're full of it. You're just upset."

"And you're disrespectful." The captain coughed his way back to an authoritative tone. "Like your rich friend."

"D'you see Sawtell come down after we got in?" Topher asked suddenly.

"No. Looking for news about his brother, you mean? No."

"Because somebody must've told him to run after me. I talked to him, but I didn't tell him anything."

"What was there to tell?"

"You know. What you and I were just saying."

"What? What news did you have?"

"Not news. Only that—you know, about the guys at the hong. That I didn't know if what the stoker told me Ol said was true or if what you said . . . Well, I didn't know anything. So I didn't say."

"But I just *told* you!" the captain wailed. "It was that snide little supercargo! *He* knew their plan! Did Sawtell ask him? He's the only one who would know! You're wrong to have no respect for me!" He was shouting. "You're wrong! I'm a decent man! I do everything for you! You should respect me, even if . . . in many ways . . . I fail."

"All right. All right. All right. Shh, captain. Shh . . ." After a silence, a smile, a lazy ripple formed on Topher's face. He murmured, "He *is* strange." He started to laugh, which echoed in the steel-lined room. "If I tell you—something weird . . ."

The sea repeated the boy's ripple of a smile. The *Myrrha* dipped. The captain felt it in his gut—overwhelming tenderness for his young friend. He knew he wasn't going to like what he was about to hear. Tears crept horizontally along crevices at the outer corners of his eyes. "Something weird about the supercargo?" he murmured poutily. Ever so slowly the tears doubled back along gutters of flesh under his baggy *cernes*. Though he couldn't make himself small, the captain lowered his chin shyly, and his features seemed to shrink against inflating pink jowls.

"Right. About him," Topher said. He pointed to the gash on his temple. "Because of this, I was bleeding a lot . . ."

"Mm. Head wound. Bleeds profusely."

"Yeah, but the thing is, he got some of the blood on his hand."

"He did that to you!"

"No. No. He was trying to help. He can be kind of—nursey, actually. He was checking out my eyes or something." Laughter interrupted him for a moment. "So he had this blood on his hand. And the—whatever—this accident I had was over with, and we had to push the cart with his shit the rest of the way to the hotel. When we start pushing he turns away from me a little. He thought I couldn't see, but I did. He turns his head like this and *licks* the blood off his hand."

The captain frowned, bewildered rather than amused or angry.

Topher said, "Strange. But maybe he was just trying to clean his hand up."

"No. You're right. It *is* strange. Like an animal."

Topher burst into laughter again. "Maybe he's, like, a vampire! That's what I almost started thinking for a second. I couldn't figure it out."

"Obviously, he *is* a vampire," the captain said gravely. "Just not because of the blood. Not literally, I mean. But that is a very odd thing to do."

"That's what *I* thought," Topher said with childish emphasis.

"Topher," the captain began. Firmly, he decided, "Don't see him anymore. I don't think you should see him anymore. There are, you know—well, of course, you know—" the captain was looking very deeply at the middle of Topher's chest, as if through the axial scar to his heart. "There are some truly fucked-up people around. I mean psychopaths and . . . crazy people, who come to a country like this where nobody cares about anybody, and they can get away with . . ." The captain began to weep.

"He's not dangerous, captain. I know. I can tell."

Nothing could stop the captain's crying. It had happened once or twice before. He quivered, and the metal cot squeaked and the head bar knocked against the bulkhead. He was losing his balance, already thrown off by drink. He was afraid of tipping backward on to the mattress, because the metal mesh underneath would certainly break. So he slid forward onto the floor, fold upon fold of him rippling off the bed in slow peristalsis. It was a sign of his tremendous distress. It was going to be an awful chore for him to get up off the floor later. For now, he sank, overwhelmed. Topher sprang up and pushed the cots apart to make room. "On your back, captain," he warned. If the man came to rest on his side or stomach and fell asleep, he might actually suffocate.

The captain was smitten by his life's long and total sterility. Sometimes depression strikes like this with biblical grandeur. Through tears and mucus, he argued aloud, "But I did love the captain!"

"Breathe!" Topher urged.

"And you, Tophe. Of course. Always."

"You're not dying."

And he wasn't. Face and jowls slick with tears and sweat, he slept, breathing unhealthily. Topher found a pillow for his head, loosened his shirt. He aligned a cot next to the captain's body and lay face down at the edge.

He chewed a nail in worry and felt a stinging at his thumb when he drew blood. He put the thumb in his mouth. Without the least fastidiousness about sweat or flab, he rested his other hand on the captain's belly, which rose above the level of the cot. That way he could monitor—quite distantly through the fat—the captain's shallow breathing. Shaking a fly from his thigh, then from his butt, humping the mattress a few times, twisting his bleeding thumb tightly in a corner of the rough sheet, Topher was sure he'd never fall asleep.

A moment later, on guard still, he was unconscious. Punch-drunk flies lapped the moist salts from his skin and the captain's.

6

SOMEWHERE AROUND NINE or ten—I thought it was the shower pipes again, but the pounding was gruffer, and it rose and fell—helicopters. B had fallen. The insurrection was taking hold in the country. Alejandrina was in turmoil. Oddly, because open fighting had been anticipated for so long, heightened alarm came with a paradoxical hint of relief. Whereas yesterday the city had been particularly quiet, people fretting behind closed doors, today markets and chandlers and cocoa rooms opened, and the streets were busier. Everywhere you saw the bright silks of Mandarin exiles' retainers and their gauze-curtained palanquins. But a superficial ordinariness hardly offset the real turmoil, which was political, even conceptual.

Now that the crisis had come, the political factions and the

subtle tides of power looked more hopeless than ever. Over the
past months, as life upriver became untenable, the Mandarins had
been gradually evacuating their households, their treasures, their
religious icons, their entire elaborate microculture to the capital.
As of today their historical presence in B was over. Alejandrina,
with its commercial links to the outside world, had always been
the drab business center, B the cultural capital. Now the two com-
munities were uneasily combined.

Besides that, troops from a regional defense league, an out-
growth of an economic cooperation treaty, had long been
deployed on the outskirts of the city. They were feared and mistrusted. ECOCOL was the Economic Cooperation League, and
the Economic Cooperation League Military Group was called
ECOMILG. ECOMILG was under the nominal authority of the
government, but through "national liaison advisers" the companies ran it. The companies had so much leverage because they'd
arranged UN-backing for ECOMILG, including the deployment
of the helicopter fleet. The companies prevented the government
from using ECOMILG or poorly equipped national forces to crack
down on opposition political parties or to establish military rule.
Some argued the companies' first-world squeamishness was what
allowed the insurrection to spread. Many who knew ECOMILG
to be bullying and poorly controlled were just as happy to have
limits put on their police powers.

With the Mandarins' final abandonment of B, their guard
troops were being evacuated by the ECOMILG helicopter fleet.
What did it mean? No one understood the tangle of favors, resent-
ments, obligations, rivalry and power among the Mandarins, the

companies and the government. But no one was happy about having yet another army in Alejandrina. There was already too much power on the ground, a near vacuum at the top.

Gossip was rife about what was happening in B. Apparently the Mandarins had left one guard division behind, mostly foreign mercenaries, with instructions to make accommodations with one or several of the competing insurrectionist groups. This backhanded pitch for cease-fire was doomed, if the bloodier-minded fanatics were in the ascendant as people said. These more radical groups were supposedly ignoring Rapithwin (the paramount idol of the dispossessed they claimed to be fighting for), because the Sultan had endorsed the status quo ante in one of his broadcasts from beyond the grave. Cynics everywhere were sure Rapithwin's electromagnetic spirit had been moved by fear of a government crackdown in the capital region. After the Sultan's craven broadcast, schism seemed possible. Today Rapithwin was speaking ambiguously in what some Alejandriniotes believed was ominous code. Rapithwinist dishwashers and litter-bearers swore it was gibberish.

That first day, I was prudent and didn't leave the hotel. I ate the terrible sandwiches from the machine in the lobby and sat and smoked at my window as the helicopters came and went overhead. I was able to buy one of the local papers from someone who'd finished it and needed change for a *maté* soda. There were several smudged halftones of events in B yesterday, a picture of the executions and one of a mob around an alarmed-looking white château captioned, "After the happy evacuation of personnel the rampage burst into the consular quarter."

On the inner pages, a rogues' gallery of narrow-eyed minis-
ters and grinning, coiffed company reps (Mandarins didn't allow
themselves to be photographed) illustrated perfectly how power
was divided into tiny, stubborn parts. To me, the most interesting picture was a group shot captioned " 'Mandarin' porte-parole,
security chief, staff and advisors." In the last row was a round
boyish face I was sure was Van Loon's. I'd have to find out if he had
any influence. I might need a powerful friend. Because the paper's
main story was particularly alarming.

On the front page it was reported that a huge treasure belong-
ing to one of the companies, unknown or unnamed, was rumored
to have fallen into the hands of insurrectionists. The treasure,
U.S.$200,000 in gold, was large enough to equip a force for a
serious assault on Alejandrina, if secret supply lines existed, or
could be set up quickly, to procure weapons. This item should
have terrified everyone in the city. Few believed it. I was one of
two—no, three—outside Anders Willis who knew the story was
true and that the whole skeptical, rumor-mad, cocksure, sarcas-
tic, glowering population could be whispering on their graves.

Enough information about me was probably on the streets.
I felt sure I'd be sought out for questioning, perhaps prevented
from leaving the country. If there was even a remote chance Van
Loon could smooth my way, I wanted us to be friends. But I had
no idea how to reach him.

I started weaning myself from the hotel the next day. I knew I'd
have to leave my treasure in its hiding place in order to do what
I had to do. Still, the nervousness that came over me when I left
was overwhelming at first. I found a dingy cocoa room within

sight of the Colebart's mossed columns and crumbling pediment. Named for their cold climate cousins, cocoa rooms here served tepid fruit drinks and Cokes and coffee. Old men whiled away the days in them. I had to wait until the pushy crowds thinned around two open copies of the newspaper, but I was finally able to crane my neck and see that the big story today was the citywide debate over whether yesterday's big story was true. And was it a gas explosion or a missile or a bomb that destroyed a feather exporter's warehouse?

As I drank coffee and steeled myself to hunt for a way out of Alejandrina, I listened to rumors about refugees from B discussed in portentous whispers. Apparently the refugees were being sequestered in a huge camp in the Alejandrina's barren eastern quarter. The government feared infiltration by terrorists from B. As always with thankless or controversial work, the companies had ceded authority over refugee affairs to the inept government, offering them an ECOMILG detachment as jailers and a thank-you.

One man in the cocoa room was particularly distraught. He turned out to be a tallow chandler from a shop down the street. His friends were trying to comfort him, but he couldn't keep back the tears after returning a second time from the refugee camp. Twice he'd been unable to get an asthmatic nephew from B released. One of the comforting friends kept giving me dark looks. I figured he was guarding the tallow chandler's privacy, so I looked away. But the man surprised me. He came over and asked with touching humility whether I thought I, an obvious foreigner, might have better luck getting the nephew out of the camp. As many of Alejandrina's older generation still did, he made a

traditional, oratorical gesture as he spoke, an arm sweeping to
the wretched chandler behind him, whose tearful gaze rested on
me—black pebbles in a shallow brook—until I said I'd try. I'd
meant to go to the government and company buildings around
the port to look for a way out of the country. People warned
me these were mobbed, unapproachable. Maybe I'd find a more
accessible or helpful official at the refugee camp, and I could per-
form a humanitarian service at the same time.

I went by cab, an extravagance costing $1.75 thanks to the
gasoline shortage, but I thought a grand entrance would be more
persuasive. We were stopped at a roadblock when we were still
out of sight of the camp. The armed boys at the roadblock were in
civilian clothes but wore new-looking claret national army berets.
There were no ECOMILG in sight, only a single policeman sitting
in a hut. I asked to speak to him. He came over, making sure I saw
his predatory smile evaporate with spooky abruptness.

He trampled over my greeting with a series of insistent questions of his own. He asked to see my passport. "It's at the hotel,
of course. I'm staying at the Hilton." I felt I was in a dangerous
position. ECOMILG were bad enough. These boys belonged to
some petty warlord loosely attached to the government. A little
too quickly I shrugged. "Well, if I can't go on, I can't."

After a pause to impress his intimidating humorlessness on
me (the country was full of talent in that art) and during which
I kept my own expression rigidly amiable, almost clownish, he
confirmed, "You can't."

I had the cabbie drop me at the port, which was teeming with
ECOMILG. I walked to the Chain Locker to check the posting

for outbound and inbound ships. The list had been moved indoors and covered with plastic, because it kept being defaced by political graffiti. The *Torres*; the *General Ashton* (both weeks away, if ever); the *Narses* (formerly the *Luv-Mee*)—no crew, no date; the *Leuconoe*—no crew, no date; and so on. The place was crowded. The sailors laughed when they saw me peering at the schedule. "Nothing but outbound—*if* they can get a crew."

I told them it looked to me like there were plenty of sailors around.

"Here, yeah. There's a lot of us here, but they won't come here, give us full pay."

It turned out they were, in effect, hiding. If they were hired at the Chain Locker they were sure to be paid. With the whiff of lawlessness in the air, crimps had become especially active on the waterfront. Rumor said they were being offered a premium to round up crews. Asked why the premium wasn't given to crewmen as an inducement to sign, the sailors nodded sagely at the ineffable logic of paymasters and said, "Why indeed? Never happens."

The oppressed gaiety of the sailors couldn't hide their genuine fear of the crimps' dire interest in naifs and drunks and any man without his papers in order. No one wanted to be on a ship that resorted to crimps. The ghouls were reputed to have an unerring eye for the friendless, anyone who would never be missed.

7

THE PROBLEM OF contacting Van Loon was solved by him. Coming back from the cocoa room across the street the next morning, I saw him. His whole upper body leaned over the Colebart desk as he spoke quietly to the day clerk. He straightened and hit the desk cheerfully. "And here he is now!"

It must not have been very hard to track down a foreigner. There were only a few of us in the city. "I thought you said some— some other place, but who cares?"

He shrugged quickly, realizing I'd lied on purpose. "I'm glad I found you." Shooting the day clerk an ambiguous look, he ushered me away from the desk to a pair of armchairs, leather-upholstered deco slabs beyond the vending machine. He sat as far forward as he could in one and explored the dings in a black-painted coffee table with a forefinger. "Ever heard of *Varanath Prin*? Or THE *Varanath Prin*? I'm not sure. Funny part of speech, 'the.' Who ever heard of a language with no articles? Apart from Latin, I guess," he caught himself. "But this isn't Indo-European or Indo-anything or Ugaritic or you-name-it. Like Basque maybe. Nobody's ever figured out where the mandarins got their language. Not 'Mandarin' obviously." He looked around him. "This used to be the best place in town a million years ago. All that woodwork is teak. Too bad nobody cares anymore."

"I saw your picture in the paper the other day . . ." I began. He was already nodding. "You work for the Mandarins?"

Still nodding, not at all fazed, he explained, "Very, very informally. A little bit. As a kind of a consultant. But completely independent. Remember, I was the one who told you we decided they were at fault in B." He waved away the need to defend himself. "But yes. I am trying to help them. You noticed that photograph? No Mandarins, not a single one. They need outsiders so they can get things done in the world."

"Because the culture's so restrictive."

"Exactly. And not always admirable."

"Executions."

"Exactly. I don't like that at all, but I'm working with them anyway." He set his boyish face at the irreconcilability of it. "You heard about the money?"

I nodded.

"Incredible. Inept! This country is so fucking unlucky. You didn't hear anything about the gold up there, did you—before we got out?"

I shook my head, then said, "Can I ask if this is part of your work? Talking to me, I mean. Don't get me wrong. I'm glad you found me, too, but I'm anxious to leave Alejandrina."

"Oh, that's no problem. I can take care of it. The other part . . ." He put his fist to his chin. His eyes peered into the blackness of the table and he appeared to think hard. "Maybe. Yes, maybe this does have something to do with my work. I'm very interested in finding out what happened, even more now this missing fortune's involved. And, yes, I guess that information could be valuable."

"So you want to have that chat we talked about."

"I do. Yes. But not only that. I also have something unpleasant—"

"Wait. Let me ask you first. How can you arrange getting somebody out of the city? I just checked on outbound ships. There wasn't anything."

"Not a problem. I'll know a little bit before—like twenty-four hours—before anything interesting gets posted, becomes general knowledge. Like when ships are ready to sail, when there's room aboard. Doesn't mean we won't have to wait some, but . . ."

"You're trying to leave yourself?"

"I think so."

"What was the unpleasant thing?"

"Mmm." He found it difficult to say. "Sure you don't want to hear about the hunt first?"

"Hunt?"

"That's *Varanath Prin*."

"What was the unpleasant thing?"

"They found a dead body."

I thought he meant Topher. The fear wrung my insides—though

I let nothing show. Emotion was at the very point of blossoming into some astonishing clarity about myself and the boy, when I realized I'd made a mistake.

Van Loon said, "They think it might be the old guy from the hong."

"Who? Ol? Fuck."

"But they don't know. They really aren't sure. Nobody knows him."

"Some of the sailors must. He had a seaman's ticket. From before he worked at the hong."

"Can't find anybody."

"You must've seen him yourself."

He shook his head. "Not to remember. I'm sure we could round up somebody eventually, but you . . . I'm sorry, if this is hard—"

"I didn't really know him. What happened?"

"Probably just drowned. *If* it's him. Some guy told them 'maybe.' But you knew him—"

"No. I was only there a couple of days. He helped me get my stuff out."

"But you'd at least remember . . ."

The morgue was full. Van Loon told me there'd been a lot of political killings recently, very little talked about. It was considered safer not to know the dead, so the place filled up, and the overflow went to the waterfront warehouse of a bankrupt meatpacking company. A balky thermostat in the biggest meat locker was proving difficult to regulate. Bodies not quickly claimed were frozen solid.

Mulish orderlies debated who'd have to carry the body out of the locker, which caused a delay. Apparently there were seven bodies inside on aluminum stretchers. The orderlies had no gloves and didn't like touching the aluminum even with hands wrapped in T-shirts or tourist sarongs. They explained sourly that a few times the cold had burned so badly they lost their grip, the load slid out of control, and body parts shattered on the floor. I caught them smiling to themselves at this gruesome exaggeration. The orderlies decided I could lean into the locker. When I did, the intense cold seemed to grab hold of my ears.

It was Ol. I'd been nervous I wouldn't recognize him. The responsibility seemed tremendous, and when I'd prepared myself by trying to remember what he looked like, all I could call to mind was his resentful red stare. In the end he didn't look like himself, but I knew it was him. He looked better than ever. His complexion had smoothed out. The bulging creases of his face and even his nose had deflated some, so he appeared, if not exactly ascetic, intelligent and more decided than he'd been in life. Death's sobriety gave him a formidable something. The ice crystals glinting from his just-open mouth and eyes lent the white, daydreaming face an air of contempt. I pulled my head back after a second and felt cold long after the locker door was closed.

From the makeshift morgue Van Loon and I went to the Chain Locker. Since his seaman's ticket entitled him to space, Ol had kept some things there. When I mentioned this, Van Loon wanted to investigate. A pot-bellied retiree at a steel desk happily refused to give us the time of day. He said he didn't know Ol, didn't know us, and wasn't about to open a locker on our say-so. Van Loon raised his voice, managing to sound friendly, all the same. "Come on! Come on!" he cried. "I'm telling you this guy knew him!" He gestured at me. "Friends, *friends*, you know? We don't want to take anything. We just want to see."

With stolid enjoyment the retiree folded his hands on his belly and said, "You show me a paper says he's dead. I got to have the paper. Then you can watch me open her up if you want, but it all goes for auction, what's inside."

"You're a stubborn fool!" Van Loon said. Even that came out like a caressing compliment.

The retiree smiled.

Van Loon and I moved aside. He was worked up, and I asked why it mattered at all to get a look at Ol's things. He took me outside. A porch ran around the Chain Locker. Some of the mahogany benches taken out of the *Myrrha* had been installed facing the streets and the harbor. Now they were covered with the carved doodles and profanities of sailors. We sat where we couldn't be overheard. Van Loon folded his arms and said nothing for a while. His face twitched in irritation when a downpour suddenly started. The noise increased our privacy. We seemed to be surrounded by curtains of living glass. "It sucks that he was the only one to get out of the hong. And now he's dead."

"Out of Bottom hong. The Anders Willis place," I stalled.

"Right. Except for you. But you didn't work there. It's strange."

"Are you saying it could be suspicious? He could've been, say— somebody could've killed him? He was a big drunk, you know."

"I know. No, supposedly there was no sign of anything . . . Unless maybe he struggled with a crimp and fell in."

"But that wouldn't be a real murder, a purposeful one, I mean."

"I never said it was. It's bad he's dead is all. Bad for me. You're not upset the way I'm talking? I don't want to sound completely coldhearted."

"I really didn't know him."

"We trust each other, right?" Van Loon asked abruptly. He smoothed his graying ginger curls. At certain angles I noticed only his face's baggy signs of age. When he looked at me directly, the full light changed him back into the boy he must once have been. His candid expression gave him an owlish look. I couldn't understand what made him push his way into other people's business. I wondered whether his energy, his air of feeling in the right were truly admirable qualities in the end. He seemed the bright, athletic, always-in-the-right kid the whole world admires. He was missing some obscurely sad or twisted quality I always looked for in people, as if I were a healer or a predator. "I'm convinced it was Anders Willis that lost the money," he said. "I've talked to them. So fucking corporate. But the person they had me talk to and the way they acted . . . That's why you've got to tell me if you remember hearing anything about it when you were up there."

I felt I couldn't trust him. I shook my head.

"You're still upset about what happened, aren't you?" he asked.

"Maybe without it registering. A little," I admitted. "The old guy helped me with some baggage of mine is all. I hardly saw him at the hong."

He put his hand on my knee, which I didn't like. I held still, though, not wanting to seem a freak, panicking and jerking at the least gesture of human kindness—assuming that's what he meant by the hand and a very flat look. "And nobody else talked about it? The gold? Because—see—it might explain why they had to stay. You told me they were supposed to come. But if they were protecting something that important . . ."

"Why wouldn't they try to load it on the *Myrrha* and come along?"

"Maybe there wasn't any time."

"Wouldn't the boat have waited?" I said.

He shrugged. I wasn't going where he wanted.

I asked him, "Do you think Ol could have brought something out? Is that why you want to get at his locker?"

"Who knows?" There was a touch of impatience in his voice.

"Look," I said. "How are you so sure it was at Bottom? There were also guys who stayed behind next door. Or got caught there. I played poker with them a couple of days before. They—or you didn't see, did you? They killed them over there. They killed Hale, anyway, a kid I played with. But maybe Cricket's crew had something big to protect. Why not?"

"That's Matheson Dixwell?"

"Yeah."

"The gold?"

"Yeah."

"No. It wasn't them." Van Loon shook his head.

"How do you know?"

Van Loon ignored the question and frowned. "Why *wouldn't* they try to get it out on the *Myrrha*?"

"Did you talk to the captain?"

"I will."

"How do you know it wasn't Matheson Dixwell?"

"Well, their godowns were destroyed, for one thing. Somebody told me."

"That doesn't mean a thing. Could've been in the hong. Or a fire might even help break open a strong room, if they did have it in a godown."

"No, no. It wasn't that." He didn't want to bother with argument. He knew something more. "We trust each other?" he repeated.

"I said so before."

"Yesterday, I was back up as far as Rapithwin's pier. The monks are acting as a sort of conduit. News and pictures come through them. It's delicate, but some of the insurrectionists are interested in talking to the Mandarins about things they don't want to get back to the companies or government. Like, 'We have a treasure. It's gold, it's this large, and we found it here. Are you interested in negotiating? Why don't we talk?' They don't want the companies or the government or, obviously, ECOMILG to know the who, what and where. Otherwise, *boom*."

I cocked my head at him. "Why so coy?"

He shrugged.

"What's to keep me from telling somebody at one of the companies now that I know?"

"They've probably figured it out by this time. And if not, who's to say they'd believe you? They're remarkably stupid. Stupid to lose so much in the first place."

"I know they had dresses at Bottom. Tea caddies, the usual crappy china, some sugar. They had a lot in that godown. Worth something even without gold."

He made a frustrated face. "They're not the types to go into business."

When the rain stopped, Van Loon arranged for a Mandarin friend to call the harbormaster, who called the morgue and the pot-bellied retiree. Van Loon and I returned triumphantly to the chain locker. The lock was attacked with a gigantic set of clippers, and the steel loop gave like wire. I had a pang of anxiety about my treasure, secured by nothing more than rope and Masonite. I'd been away from it most of the day.

Inside Ol's locker were a heavy slicker, useless in this climate, a marlinspike, a shoe box containing photographs, a convex-convex lens, a roll of electrical tape, and two cheap alarm clocks missing batteries. There was also some clothing on a hook and a votive candle in a tin pannikin.

"I'd like to have that," I said.

"What? The pannikin?" the retiree snapped. He examined it for a long time. Ol or someone had scratched a pattern around the outside. It was dented, worthless. "Got to wait for the auction."

"Come on. He was a friend," Van Loon tried.

"You mean to pay?" the man asked me.

"Sure. I'll give you a dollar."

Van Loon rolled his eyes.

"Ought to wait for the auction," the man grumbled.

"He was a friend!" Van Loon repeated. "He shouldn't have to pay at all. A dollar's crazy!"

"Shut up," I said. "I'll give you a dollar. I want to have it."

The man shrugged, and I handed him silver for the tin cup.

•   •   •

TOPHER SMITH HAD phoned me three times at the Colebart.
I tried the number he left, but no one answered. His last message
said he might stop by "Society" that night and gave an address
close to the hotel. When the day clerk handed me the three slips
of paper, he smirked and subtly pointed with his nose at the message on top, the one with Society's address. He said it was a strip
club. But I had no intention of not spending the evening next to
my treasure. I'd been away too long, all day.

Strange to say, as the hours passed, I couldn't get into that
familiar state of existence in which I was happy to zone out beside
my treasure like a rich troll under a bridge. A little interaction
with Van Loon must have given me the taste for humanity. Or Ol's
icy face, a *memento mori* now fixed in mind, made it too terrifying
to pass time doing nothing but waiting. I smoked a cigarette at the
window of my room, using Ol's pannikin with a bit of water in it
as an ashtray. The ash kept hitting the water with the miniaturized
sound of a flimsy godown collapsing in flames.

My window looked out over the Colebart's colonnade. I watched
them close up the cocoa room I'd been going to each day. Gray-
painted shutters, which acted as awnings when open, were lowered one by one over the windows until the place had a completely
unwelcoming look. A few old-timers shuffled out, but others shuffled in. After a while a small red neon sign—B A R—was lit.

When I finally went down, I realized this was the place. I'd
already found it without knowing it, which made me smile at my
luck. Under the neon sign, a name was painted on one of the gray
shutters in laborious red cursive, quite small: *Societé des Ambianceurs*

et des Personnes Elegantes. It was almost entirely dark out now, but over the harbor the tail end of a dusky sunset, partly hidden by a rakish scarf of cloud, glowed like a brazier. In the time it took me to glance at it, the seeming embers went gray.

Inside the cocoa room, or "Society," a few people went through the sluggish routine of setting up. Besides me, there were only four customers. Two were heavy, bleary older men in jeans, one wearing a souvenir sweatshirt, "Key West" under a palm tree, the other in a freshly starched, untucked striped oxford. Each made a little home of the part of the counter where he sat, arranging money, ashtray, cigarettes, lighter and drink just so and strenuously ignoring his mirror image doing the same. Two younger men chuffed on and on in a conversation that was all uproarious whispers. A slinky, elegant guy whom I took to be the Congolese who ran the night shift here, ferried coffeemakers and newspapers attached to oak staffs into a back room. He came out with heavy plywood cubes and arranged them in rows against two walls. No one paid any attention to three boys wearing only sneakers and skimpy sateen shorts, or in one case, even skimpier work clothes. One stood on the bar stuffing his street clothes and wallet into a cranny above a pipe. Another did the same where the tall liquor cabinet left a little space between the top shelf and the low, black-painted ceiling. The third boy bobbed in the bustling Congolese's wake begging for something or explaining something, either way unconvincingly. I couldn't hear much of what he said, but I found his lying—enthusiastic and obviously bald-faced—appealing, even up-front.

The boy gave up, smiled at me, slouched on to a chair next to mine and said, "I hate this place." I bought him a drink, which he sipped through tiny red cocktail straws. He was slight, bony and tanned and had a dazzling but empty smile that spread across his face like oil poured in a copper skillet. He'd come into town with a load of wool from Riverina and had just lost his first job as a waiter at a fishhouse. When I told him I was waiting for somebody, he did a one-second travesty of pouting, then went off, rubbing past me like a cat, promising, "I'll be back. You're exactly my type."

By stages the place got busier. A few more dancers ran in late, lobbed shoulder bags to the bartender and emerged from a back room wearing doubled-up thongs. Standing on one of the cubes, a dancer twisted backward to check a classically pale butt for blemishes or a scratch, brushed it lightly, tugged the front of the thong lower to show a good stretch of shaved pubes, and started dancing, scanning the dim room for familiar faces, before his own settled into the vacant, countrified expression of a guy hoping to be met at a north Georgia bus station. The dancers cycled from cube to cube or strolled among the customers. They weren't self-conscious being naked, even down on the floor, but they held themselves with an absorbed daintiness, because, wearing no clothes, they could easily be scratched by a watch's winding knob or a ring or burned by a cigarette end. And, in a sense, their skin was their fortune.

Seeing Topher walk in caused me the keenest pleasure, not that I'd been bored or unhappy or even uninterested watching the boys lightly, almost symbolically, caress their ribs and crotches as they danced. I'd moved to a quieter spot near the door and sat in a kind of high chair at a round table hardly bigger across than a stool. Topher saw me but didn't come over.

I could read the sweetness underneath. He was trying to maintain a quirky frown of dignity as he nodded to an older man he knew and to the bartender, who screamed, "Ah, siren song of the lower depths bringing him home! You're not thinking of dancing, are you? Gotta talk to Ronnie." Two of the boys up on cubes gave Topher drowsy nods, rising from their low level of existence like sleepers mulling over a suspicious noise for just a moment. A third boy hopped down from his cube and gave Topher a hug and showed off new sneakers. They conferred in whispers for a moment.

Then Topher came over to me, trying to hold on to the cool-guy frown and almost succeeding. He tossed a heavy canvas bag onto the other chair. When the chair tottered, his hand darted out to steady it, which spoiled the casual effect. Frowning for real, he sat and mentioned, "I hardly come here anymore, but now I see it again I wonder if I hate it. I bet you think it's sort of—low."

"Not really. I feel at home here." It was a place like this where I'd first met Dadi Anton.

Topher smiled as if he thought I were crazy. I got him a drink and we sat for a while, looking at each other, but not into each other's eyes and not without long breaks. I don't think he realized I often won't look at people at all. Nervous about my silence or my wandering eyes, he pulled several books from the canvas bag and told me he'd been trying to sell them to book dealers. He didn't really want to, because they were gifts from the captain, but he needed the money. I promised I wouldn't inform on him. Still, like a father ("for chrissakes"), I grilled him about the twenty I'd given him What happened to that? It was like pulling teeth. He tried to distract me with the books. Then he admitted he'd given the money to his father. "You told me you ran away a long time ago." I said. I sounded a little prosecutorial, making it seem like he was lying.

"I did. I did," he said. "Just sometimes I have to help him. He really needs it more than me."

"He ripped you off, right?"

"No! Now, will you look at these?"

"I'm not going to buy any books."

"Not to buy. Just look."

I felt his eyes on my face as I shuffled through them. It was a weird collection. A cheap, locally published guide to Alejandrina, a paperback called *Simulating Terrorism* (I had to open that one to figure out it was textbook of law enforcement exercises), volume two of a history of terrorism, called *War in the Shadows*, and a huge, illustrated history of art.

He smiled as if I had to be flabbergasted. "Thought I was dumb, didn't you?"

"I didn't. But who would ever buy this crap?"

"I'm interested in a lot of things," he bragged. He took the two terrorism books. "Actually these are worth a lot around here. But they could get us in trouble." He tucked them back into the canvas bag. "You should take me seriously," he muttered, more coy than offended.

"I do. I admit I'm a little surprised. But the terrorism stuff seems—not exactly what this country needs. More violence. I hate that. That Van Loon character has got me roped into going hunting tomorrow. I've never been hunting, but I have a feeling I won't like that either. *Varanath Prin*. It's some Mandarin thing."

He almost fell off his chair. He was exaggerating his shock, but you really could fall off those high chairs and he nearly had, and it wasn't part of a performance. When his hand came down on the big art book for balance, the table tipped and the drinks sloshed. "I can't believe I'm talking to you!" Mouth agape in a pantomime of disbelief, "I can't believe I'm even talking to you." His expression looked comical. I was smiling. I didn't understand that for him exaggeration didn't mean you weren't being serious. "You— you come to this country . . . You—like—you hang out with the Mandarins—fuck!—you hang out with the *Mandarins*—"

"Are you messing around with me?" I asked.

"No! I'm serious. I can't believe it. You're like a—I don't know—you're like—the oppressor."

"Topher," I said casually. "I didn't mean to cause offense. But I have to get out of the city, and the only way is to suck up to Van Loon, the guy that invited me."

"Who is he?"

"Some guy who works for them. He didn't seem all bad. Except he's the one who called you a lowlife."

"Probably saw me in here. Some cheapskate prick." He shook his head at me. "I'm so—I'm so shocked. I guess you're not at all like I thought you were."

"Don't be ridiculous. I hardly know the guy. And anyway you can't judge a person by who they hang around with."

Now I was concerned. He looked truly unhappy. Maybe tearful, though I couldn't be sure in the dim red light. For a second I thought he was going to stand up and leave. When I tried to say something, he held up his hand, shook his head and whispered,

"Shut up!" to his lap. He slid the art book to his knees and rapidly leafed through red masterpiece after red masterpiece, red *Raft of the Medusa*, red *Nocturne in Black and Gold*, red *Departure from Cythera*, red *Socrates Drinking Hemlock*.

I started to relax. "I'm sorry, but I have to get out of the country. It's business," I explained again gently.

"I don't think you have normal feelings. I think you're decadent."

The word made me angry for some reason. "I'm not decadent. Of course I have feelings. Haven't I just been saying I'm sickened by all the violence in this—by this whole country? I don't know why anyone, you included, would want to stay here. To be perfectly honest, you're the only appealing or decent—"

"I'm not a thing."

"I wasn't going to say *thing*."

"Yes, you were." He laughed so brightly his air of grief and disapproval vanished. He'd stopped on a red *Doubting Thomas* by Hendrik ter Bruggen. "Here's a guy with a disgusting scar. Ugly sucker."

For a second I was annoyed at Topher—or was it at myself?—because he was a kid, a stupid kid. His red cheek, even with half-formed zit and straggling blond whiskers, had amazing authority over me. I suppose everybody is fundamentally mysterious. But there are some whose mystery so aggravates you, an aggravation like love, that you imagine dismantling them piece by piece. This act of destruction, however fantastic, upset me when the object in question was, as he'd pointed out, not a thing but a person—someone barely formed intellectually or emotionally, someone who couldn't recognize Jesus, never mind Hendrik ter Bruggen.

The more violent it felt just looking at his cheek or thigh or thumb, the more "good" he seemed to me in the sentimental Jesus sense. I knew he was an ordinary kid. But the geometry between us was somehow ideal, like the unique spot under a three-acre dome where a whisper echoes perfectly. I assumed my feelings were all echo, not love, and that I was basically alone when I was with him. I thought the opposite was true for him. For him, it was love, we were together, and I was real.

I sighed and murmured, "I'm sorry." Out loud, apparently.

"What are you sorry about now?"

"I thought I hurt you."

"How?" He smiled.

"I thought my thoughts hurt you."

"That would be weird," he said like an American teenager. His face clouded. "You know . . . I don't know if I should tell you . . ."

We seemed to be the only two in the room who were, in a way, up at the surface. Everyone else had dived deep, as deep as possible, to the deepest level of existence. There was no self-conscious slumming, nor any giggly neophytes at Society. No matter how drunk, the men all watched the stoned dancers with the most urgent sobriety. True, the one wearing the "Key West" sweatshirt smiled and made a remark, while he was rubbing a folded bill between one kid's ass cheeks, but as soon as the bill was spent for good, he reverted to divine stupor. You realized his smile and the remark were a sham. The low, low, inexpressive being was the actual man.

"Tell me what?" I asked Topher. "Go ahead. We trust each other, right?"

"I'm not sure," he said, looking me in the eye. "I do have a problem with you. Actually a big problem, but I don't want to think about it."

"This problem is what you're not sure you should tell me?"

"No. What I'm not sure I should tell you is that they're going to want to talk to you at Anders Willis."

"I know that."

"Yeah, but I think it's a bigger deal now. This guy came by the *Myrrha* tonight trying to talk to the captain."

"Tall, curly-haired, a little older than me?" Topher nodded, and I said, "That's Van Loon. I was with him all day today."

"Yeah, well, the captain wouldn't talk to him about anything. So you don't have to—"

"I'm not worried. Why would I worry?"

"Afterwards, the captain said he told this guy to get out and that him and you—the captain and you—were being called in for some Anders Willis investigation about what happened in B. Captain told the guy that's why he couldn't talk to him." "I haven't heard anything about it. Probably the captain was just saying whatever to get rid of Van Loon."

"I don't think so. I think the captain's already started talking to them at Anders Willis. And I think he told them about you. You shouldn't look at it like betrayal or anything, though. You guys were thinking about talking to them anyway, right? It's probably best to get it all out in the open."

"What are you talking about? I haven't done anything wrong."

He eyed me a long time. I started to feel almost everything I'd

ever done could be looked at as wrong. It was shaming and annoy-
ing to be observed like that by a kid. But I didn't let on. He said,
"Yeah, well, this is my problem with you."

I shrugged. What was he talking about?

"It's why I don't even want to see Bill Sawtell again, cause he'll
get angry, and then maybe I'll get angry, too."

I waited.

"I heard why you guys didn't wait for the hong's crew up in
B. The captain was going to wait, but you told him the crew had
some plan to stay behind. But we don't think they did. The old
guy, Ol, even told our stoker they didn't. Which means the *Myrrha*
left just because you'd gotten your stuff on board."

I don't know why I wanted him to think it was possible. Scare
him or test him by making him wonder whether I was completely
awful? Maybe I was just irritated by his out-of-true show of
fatherly disappointment. Maybe I couldn't bear a boy's unthinking skin and muscle having so much authority over me. I didn't
deny I'd told the captain to leave, though Topher left me room to
do it. I didn't say anything.

After a long while, he went on mournfully, "I have this weird
thing where I totally lose it. I freak out. It's embarrassing.
I—like—start hitting my head against the wall. Captain says it's
a panic attack. So when it's going to happen, he gives me some
dumb chore to do. When we were about to leave B, I said, 'Fuck,
let *me* run get them!' And he told me, 'No, I know for a fact they
mean to stay. They *want* to stay.' I started freaking out about it.
Ended up, he made me polish all the brass in the pilothouse."

"Ah."

"Do you want me to—go away or something?" he asked as if he'd done something unforgivable.

"No, let's go out together," I said, smiling, hoping to cheer him up some. I paid for both of us.

"Nice night," he muttered as rats rustled up the vine-choked trunks of palms along the street. "That," he informed me in answer to my question—he was so easily cheered, like polishing brass!—"That's called the Mandarin Temple. Only it isn't." He was pointing at a small knoll on the far side of the harbor. "You'd know, if you bought my guidebook."

"Why don't you tell me? You be the guide."

We stopped at a place where the view was passable out over the harbor. The black water was spangled by the lights of fishing boats, dim ones where men ate lonely suppers, bright ones where they worked, lamps shining down into the sea to attract the hope-lessly reflexive fish into nets. On the knoll the "temple" was lit by aqua spotlights, a composition somebody probably thought glam-orous at one time. It looked tawdry.

Apparently the knoll itself, unexcavated, may have been an arti-ficial structure from the Mandarins' ancient coastal period, but the so-called temple built on top was a fake. In the early days of the foreign concession, an archaeologically-minded Englishman, Josiah Sweet, had been so taken with the Mandarins' strange cul-ture he'd produced, purely from his imagination, a temple for them. Now a picturesque ruin, it looked almost authentic and was Alejandrina's only tourist attraction. Topher emphasized that he knew it was a folly. He hadn't been taken in. With a sigh of pity he explained that even many locals believed the thing was genuine.

His mood had mostly recovered, and in a kid-like burst of enthusiasm he asked if he could show me something, a sort of surprise. He started walking. Hopelessly reflexive, I followed.

We walked a long way east, so far I began getting stares as a stranger and worried he meant to take me to the refugee camp. I admit it. I even had a flicker of doubt about Topher. We passed some nice spots for an ambush. The loping dogs glared at us like angry Bill Sawtells before dodging off with a just-audible grunt or whimper. "Where exactly—what is it you want to show me, Tophe?"

"Only a little farther, I promise," he begged.

We walked on, well into the depopulated zone. We walked until my feet were sucking at the sweat in my shoes. We'd started talking philosophy—friendship, truth, God, the purpose of life. The sort of conversation not really meant to be coherent or even remembered, logical only in shape like a ladder you use to climb someplace then kick away when you spot another ladder leading someplace else. For him the conversation may have been fresh and real and permanent. I'd had it before and knew you kicked it all away in the end.

I figured out where he was taking me a little before we got there. He wanted me to see his father's house, the house he grew up in. That's how hungry he was to be known. This neighborhood was studded with those empty balcony-fretted white buildings, and tonight it had a drained-ocean dreaminess. Topher told me no one could live in the buildings now, because "terrorists" had poured cement into the machine wells at the bottom of the elevator shaft. For government, company or anyone to recoup the value of the buildings, the elevator mechanism would first have to be chipped from concrete. Between two of these forlorn stelae was a fairly ordinary tile-roofed house. As he led me in, Topher gestured at the barred half windows of the basement he'd sometimes been imprisoned in as a child.

I think what he particularly wanted to show me but couldn't explain was that the place was tidy, well-furnished, adequately lit, comfortable. Nothing amazing, but a small domestic achievement in that city, and it was his achievement. Not bad for a runaway who slept on a mat on a riverboat and presumably only dropped in every few weeks or months. The furniture was cast-off but well maintained. A few posters on the walls were presents from friends. Without any sense of intimidation Topher threw open the door to his father's bedroom. Inside, I glimpsed a withered lump in the bed, its frightened, liquid eyes agleam—hardly the man I expected. There were no introductions. Topher and the lump exchanged ambiguous grunts. The door closed. Maybe the father was just another thing about Topher I was meant to register.

The boy pointed out his collection of books, all presents from the captain. He made coffee, drawing my attention to the coffeemaker, a used one from Society, a gift of the Congolese who ran the place. He flopped down on a small cot in the living room to show me exactly how he'd been positioned when he called the Colebart that afternoon. He writhed to show me his positions for the second and third calls as well. The house had a private phone, a rarity in Alejandrina and, again, his own small triumph over the country's sclerotic telecom bureaucracy.

Without noticing the obvious chain of thought, Topher told me he'd often called his now-lost friend, the Seventh Day Adventist, lying on the cot and looking out the window just as he was now.

The tour wasn't impressing me the way Topher hoped it would. By this time I was feeling sad, displaced, tired, a little pitying. I was anxious not to get ensnared in Topher's maudlin humor. Drily, I commented, "And now he throws rocks at you."

"I don't think it was him who threw it. I think it was that jack-ass waiter. Kid I don't even know, by the way. He's the type that gets caught up, goes along, wants people to like him."

"So you're not angry at your friend anymore? I thought you felt abandoned by him?"

"I guess some people can't help doing the wrong thing."

"What's that mean?"

"He just wants his jacket back," Topher said as if another con-versation hadn't almost risen to the surface.

"Show me?"

He shrugged, jumped up and tugged at the stumbling slid-ing door of a closet. Inside hung a lone jacket. An ordinary black motorcycle jacket with a handful of cryptic badges along one sleeve. Much too heavy for the climate.

"What was the one you gave him like?"

Relishing his guilt with a smile, Topher said, "Not as nice. By far. Really, I was going to give it back, but it's too big a deal now." He struggled to close the door on his treasure.

I knew I had to go, but with quiet, stupid insistence I stayed on, running my gaze around the place like a cat burglar in the lovemaking stage. In truth the rooms were a little sparse, tatty, depressing. The two of us kept looking at each other now. More and more his gaze anticipated my going away. I couldn't stand it, so I finally just muttered, "I've got to get going, Topher."

I was careful not to touch him before I left.

8

MANY MANDARIN RELIGIOUS celebrations were held in the coastal area, the Mandarin ancestral home. Because of the general exile from B, *Varanath Prin* would draw more people than usual despite the political situation. The date for the hunt was calculated on the Mandarins' elaborate lunar calendar—of unknown origin, like the rest of their culture.

The Mandarin year was rigorously divided into twelve full moons, a period that falls short of the solar year. This meant the beginning of the year and all subsequent dates and holidays moved slowly backward through the familiar solar year and the two tropical seasons by about 11 days per year. The conceptual subtlety of their calendar was that it applied only to them. It wasn't a universal device for measuring time. The world, they conceded, was subject to the sun and seasons. Their own illusory backward motion in time ruled the life of their souls, which grew younger as their bodies aged. They were alone among the people of earth to be moving toward the beginning of time where a paradise existed in which souls lived free of all memory.

New moons were days of fasting, unless they fell on a solstice or equinox when, instead of grieving, the Mandarins rejoiced that the moon was hiding from the influence of the sun. Full moons were holidays, each one named and changing in character depending on where it fell during the solar year. When a full moon fell on a solstice or equinox, the Mandarins mourned in accordance with the importance of the particular moon. Any full moon falling on a summer solstice was considered the worst possible omen. The cycle of time and the special status of their souls were threatened by solar domination. When the first full moon of the year fell on the summer solstice—an extremely rare event; their histories recorded three—calamity was inevitable and could only be put right by human sacrifice of staggering volume—again, according to the histories.

Looked at deeply, the calendar was astonishingly sophisticated. The Mandarins were perfectly aware of the inequality of days to year. Scorning the Julian and Gregorian shuffles, they allowed the solar year itself, the cycle of days, to drift slowly backward by about a day in four years. Yet there was never any "about" in their astronomical calculations. They'd observed how the cycle of sidereal days moved backward, as well. Balancing these supposed lunar influences on solar and sidereal time, they were further aware of the infinitesimal enlargement of the moon's orbit, its slow spiraling away from the earth and the consequent slowing of the backward motion of their lunar year. This grievous fact was associated with a sort of Twilight of the Gods myth, the possibility of their culture's doom. In other words, motion into the future, which is death.

Naturally the Mandarins were conscious of the apparent general forward motion of time regardless of all these cycles, and they attributed it to the sun. But the fact that they were the sole human culture happy to leave disengaged these natural timekeeping cycles, which can only be joined up by absurdities of mathematics, may have disposed them to think of time as authentically malleable or inhomogeneous, a deeper truth of which—and modernizing Mandarins might admit this—their retrograde lunar time was only an apt symbol.

The philosophical details of the calendar were for adepts. Most Mandarins only cared about the storied, festive changing of the months. The second, sixth and twelfth full moons were called the backward-looking moons and were specially loved. When any of them fell on a day calculated to be the midpoint between an equinox and a solstice, a very safe place for a full moon to fall, a sacrificial hunt called *Varanath* was added to the usual holiday. The twelfth moon, the current moon, was the bird moon. On the cusp of the monsoon and dry seasons its color changed from yellow (the previous year) to red (this year). So the hunt would be *Varanath Prin*, the hunt for a red bird.

Van Loon suspected that the beautiful bird in question was a Scarlet Ibis, or something closely related. It only flew short distances, usually a mere hop into the trees to avoid predators.

Otherwise it lived on the floor of the jungle near streams. It used its long bill to overturn stones and forest litter, and it fed on grubs, crawfish and insects. Van Loon told me it buried its eggs in mud.

We were jostling along in a highly decorated, mule-drawn cart, Van Loon and myself and a Mandarin guide and driver. The caravan that set out to hunt that one small bird must have included two hundred men. Our cart was one of about fourteen. Then there were palanquins and men on horseback and a large contingent on foot, including some Mandarins and a good number of their adored children, boy children only.

It was tricky not to fall into a corrupt "noble savages" way of thinking about these people. Their terra-cotta faces rarely betrayed anything but stoicism, dignity or laughter, though their uniformly dark eyes were always full of amusement, something confusingly cruel and humane at the same time. Whether they were Parsi or Malay or both, at origin, no one knew. Whatever they were, they weren't Chinese, certainly not Chinese officials—the term "Mandarin" had been used for convenience by the first Westerners in the country and only described their control over trade and the elaborate formality of their culture. They had no name for themselves at all, not even "the people" like the Inuit. Their population wasn't large. They were outnumbered many times over by the Karak Indians, who had almost no hand in the country's affairs. Everyone knew the story of the Mandarins' arrival at some point in the dim past, but some anthropologists were convinced their presence predated the arrival of the Karak Indians, whom the locals considered indigenous. Within historical memory Islamic invaders pushed the Mandarins from the coast to B. But the Islamic invaders, like the Portuguese and the Dutch who came later, were absorbed by the coastal dwellers—neither Karak nor Mandarin but an unknown people under Mandarin suzerainty up to that point. In time the invaders themselves became Mandarin subjects, or subordinate neighbors, but the Mandarins never returned to the coast.

This was Van Loon's synopsis. He was trying to make it clear to me that the Mandarin exile from B was epochal. "If they'd been able to stay, they would have tried to arrange some kind of condominium with the insurrectionists. Exactly the reason they left that mercenary division behind. And if what we hear from the monks is true, it might be working. The insurrection isn't directed at them exclusively, even if their policies set it off. Some of us have been wondering—and we're the ones working for them!—whether they didn't half collude in the insurrection when they failed to protect, to really protect, the company hongs and property. Maybe they thought it would be convenient to have the companies driven out. They look more nativist, closer to the insurrection, than the government does right at the moment. The big problem's been the airlift. The Mandarins feel obliged to the companies now. And they're beginning to suspect they were maneuvered into the airlift, because the companies wanted to break the Mandarin grip on B as much as the other way around. Maybe the companies want free rein in B for themselves some-where down the line. The Mandarins are trying to couch exile in terms of an historical return, but I have a feeling they're unhappy with the deal. There's nothing for them here."

Van Loon couldn't stop talking. He'd described the calendar, the bird, Mandarin history, and now current political machinations. He was leaning against me as he whispered. Ruts in the road kept driving his shoulder into mine and giving his speech peculiar emphases. Even so I thought he sounded nervous.

We were seated together at the back of the cart. The Mandarin guide was perched on a high bench in front, and the driver sat at his feet. Van Loon was whispering because much of what he said was controversial and best not overheard by the guide, but he didn't need to. The cart was so loud I sometimes had trouble hearing him myself. The solid wooden wheels and axle groaned. Pebbles and sand had been secreted behind gold repoussé devil's faces nailed to each wheel. They made a sound like waves as the cart moved unsteadily forward. Long bamboo poles arced rearward from the cart's back corners. Hung with bits of mirror, bells and flowers cut from sheet copper, the poles jangled constantly. The reins and mule and horses and palanquins and all the other carts were decorated just as noisily. On top of that were the widespread laughter and chattering of the Mandarins.

The crowd was as festive and carefree as any I'd ever seen. It was hard to imagine a war was on, that terrorist bombs were going off in Alejandrina, or that these people were deeply unhappy in the capital. Even when two of the carts got stuck in mud, their tackle entangled, the mishap was treated with curious lightheartedness. Shouts of alarm became laughter. The road had degenerated as we moved farther into the jungle, and here it crossed a riverbed. Men in red silks and embroidered slippers dropped their elaborately carved bows helter-skelter and leapt into the mud. One mule moaned, a hind leg sunk to the fetlock. Quivers full of painted arrows rattling on their backs, the men dragged the mule's leg free and helped push the cart across the riverbed. They laid flat stones in the mud for the other carts to drive across. Mules were whipped to a trot, and one by one the carts sped over the riverbed to laughter and cheers. Our guide nearly fell backward into our laps from his high bench, causing howls of mirth.

Our first stop was a clearing by a bend of a river in spate. It wasn't clear to me why we were stopping. What was that building of corrugated steel? Who'd cleared the jungle here? Van Loon's nervousness became more pronounced. He hardly bothered answering my questions. The more august Mandarins conferred with a knot of ECOMILG soldiers who came out of the building together with three men in sweaty T-shirts, baseball caps and heavy rubber gloves. The Mandarin caravan milled about as if a long wait were expected.

The clearing had been a Karak village, now wiped off the face of the earth. Not by ECOMILG but by some marginal guerilla force. ECOMILG had come in and taken over the day before. There were no telltale sounds, but Van Loon and I each believed something horrible was going on inside the corrugated steel building. The Mandarins didn't seem bothered in the least. They had some ill-defined rights in the area (which was called a National Park), hence the long negotiations with the ECOMILG commander. The slouching soldiers and the three men in T-shirts surveyed the circus that had come to park in the clearing with contempt. Mandarin culture was loathed as effeminate by many in the country. To the Mandarins themselves, outsiders barely existed.

"This will go on for quite a while," Van Loon warned me. To kill time we got out of the cart and wandered toward the river. "Our leader today is one of the Tarkonets, a big family and famous for being long-winded." He pointed at a kid who'd come down to the river ahead of us. "See that boy? An important boy. He's the son of one of the Tarkonets, same family."

The boy was about ten. Like most his age he carried a tiny bow of bamboo and string, as well as a stock of arrows. Normally Mandarins wore full-length robes fastened up the front with frogs. Even Van Loon was wearing an ill-fitting blue one, though I was in khaki. The robes were often partly undone in the heat, so you could see that men wore silk pants underneath, boys, loincloths. This Tarkonet boy had undone his red robe entirely and it kept dropping from his shoulders. In only a yellow loincloth he sat on a log, which turned out to be the rotting hull of a Karak canoe. With aristocratic self-possession he shot arrows—slivers of bamboo—in every direction.

The stocky Mandarin body type was surprisingly virile, kouros-like, among the very young. This boy's tiny bow exaggerated the effect. He was a miniature Apollo. He'd drawn one foot back, and his toes curled forward on a muddy swirl of red silk. Tensely he half knelt, half sat at one end of the canoe. His shoulders and arms flexed tightly when he brought the little bow alongside his placid face to aim. We could hear the dull twang of the string followed by his silvery murmur, "Bioio." Van Loon whispered in my ear, "Just the sound of a bow. Means nothing."

I turned to say something to Van Loon about the boy's breathtaking hauteur, but my remark died on my lips. Something about

the light made Van Loon look terrible, haggard. It hadn't registered
with me till now. His expression was pathetic. Sweat glittered in
hollows under his eyes, and the curls pasted to his temples were
black. I had no chance to ask what was wrong. He noticed me
looking at him and immediately began talking, teaching me as he
had been all day. "You see how everyone's wearing red? But here
and there a little yellow, like the boy? And then the old Tarkonet,
the one negotiating, he's all in yellow," he said.

"Color of the moon?"

"Right. Red this year. But the twelfth moon was yellow last
year. So high-status people will wear a bit of yellow, not because
they think the cycle of the moon should move in the other direction—forward—but because they think their souls have mastered
solar time in some small way. So they wear last year's color as if
they're moving backward in time absolutely. As for me, when the
moon moves backward through the monsoon, it'll be red again
next year, then turn blue, then green. So I wear blue now as a
token of respect, because I'm *not* Mandarin. I can't be. I'm not on
their cycle, but I acknowledge it. They notice that sort of thing. I
guess it's silly, but they adore puzzles."

"So this is gauche?" I touched my khaki pants.

I was trying to be lighthearted, but Van Loon shook his head
and said, "Of course not. You're a stranger." He folded his arms and
looked down at veins of ants crossing the packed earth path we stood
on. A drop of sweat fell from the end of his nose. "You're not going
to like this, I'm afraid. I think—I think inviting you along today was
a terrible—betrayal, almost. Why don't we arrange for you to stop
here? Maybe we can pick you up on the way back." He was grave.

"I'm not sure it would be a good idea to stay behind with that crowd," I argued. I meant the ECOMILG soldiers. "I don't know what's been going on here, but I have a bad feeling."

"Right, right," he agreed unhappily. "Jesus, I'm sorry."

"Mandarins are going to put me in a pot?"

"Don't be an idiot," he said angrily. "This isn't a joke. Somebody really is going to get killed. They like to pretend it's an execution. It's not. It's ritual murder. They always choose some mental defective. Or a debtor. I can't stand it."

EVENTUALLY THE CARAVAN got underway again, and we came to a second clearing, which the Tarkonet judged suitable for the hunt. The hunters were going to wait here instead of chasing the bird through the jungle. Beaters, impoverished taro farmers and quite a few Indians, would drive the bird into the open. They carried spikes of dried bamboo in each hand. When shaken like sistra, the bamboo leaves set up a lovely rustling. The beaters dispersed, and the rest of us loitered by another stream. Boys shot their arrows at minnows. Men knelt and scraped the now-dried mud from their robes and slippers. The hunters among them crumbled the flakes of clay between their palms, then rubbed the powder on their fingers and bowstrings. Porters and cart drivers hung back by the carts or drifted indifferently after their sly mules which grazed farther and farther into the forest. Van Loon and I drew apart, our Mandarin guide following us closely this time.

After a long wait, somebody must have heard something, because the whole mob fell silent. Smiles flashed among their faces like scallops of sunlight on the stream. In the quiet I could hear the distant rustling of bamboo. That sound was soon followed by trilling ululations from various points in the forest. The older Mandarins withdrew toward the stream, children straggling after them. The hunters fell into a rough semicircle open in the direction of the most frequent cries.

"We'll stay here," Van Loon told our Mandarin guide when the man wanted us to move closer. The man seemed disappointed.

"This was another village?" I wondered. "They just drive them off?"

Van Loon was too distracted to answer, so the guide told me, "This was no village here. This was only Karak, you know? National Park."

"There!" I couldn't help blurting out. I'd seen a rising streak of red in a patch of sunlight, a long way off. The hunters were jostling each other, or running behind the line and squeezing in where they weren't wanted.

"You see the bird? Very hard to see from here," the guide complained.

"I might just turn away or go down to the river," Van Loon whispered. "You could come, too. It'll be obvious—the moment to turn away, or not to look. Did you hear it?"

"No, not yet."

"It has an ugly voice. A squawk."

I whispered back, "Why do you dislike Topher Smith?"

"I don't," he said, genuinely confused. "Oh . . . " He remembered. "That was only—that was much more about you."

I frowned at that but hurried on. Now seemed the moment

for truth. "You went to see the captain. Did he tell you anything about B?"

"He only said Anders Willis was investigating."

"I haven't heard anything about that." My voice must have been unsteady.

"Shh," Van Loon said. "Don't worry. Of course, they want to talk to you. There. I saw it again."

"I saw it maybe," the guide echoed, sidling closer.

"What are you doing for these people, Carter?"

Van Loon shrugged. Presumably he couldn't answer with the guide standing right there.

I said, "I want to be out of Alejandrina before there's any investigation. It scares me."

"Anders Willis investigates," the guide put in, shaking his head rapidly. Van Loon and I both stared at him. The man looked back at me sympathetically. "Company! Scares me, too. Because there will be an attack on the capital soon, no? Ah, finally I saw it there. Yes, it scares me."

Van Loon was nodding sagely, not knowing what to say.

At that moment the red bird exploded from the jungle on weak wings, shrieking. It seemed to wobble in the air, not clearly a bird at all. The hunters, their sublime expressions raised to the precariously suspended bit of scarlet, ran underneath it, bows and arrows clattering. Their semicircle became a circle (with some last jostling for position). The circle moved to keep the exhausted animal at its center. With agonized hesitation the red thing drifted down.

The second it touched ground, it became a bird. Its feathers were ruffled in rage, and it appeared full of energy. The ring of hunters revolved slightly. The bird hopped back into flight in an attempt to escape. Revolving still, the circle of men ran with it, and the bird was compelled to land in their midst again. Shaking their bows, they walked it back to the middle of the clearing. It attempted to rush one or two of them on foot but was easily frightened back to the center.

When it was obvious the bird had no strength left to fly, several shouts came from the old men by the river. Out of nowhere a young Mandarin in white was led toward the circle of hunters. Or half-carried by two of the elders, since the poor man's legs bent like noodles. He was probably drugged. His expression shifted. A ghastly, idiotic smile turned to nothing—the too-aware blank-ness of a man falling from an immense height. He was shoved into the circle of hunters, who all began shouting at him. They weren't shouting in anger. It was a matter of control, the way an orderly will take command if a patient gets rowdy coming out of anesthesia. The prisoner tried to stand and walk and crawl but was shouted down every time. He couldn't manage his legs prop-erly anyway. The bird hopped around him in equal confusion. The hunters kept shouting until the man was on his knees and motion-less at the center of the ring, the bird near him.

All this time, as if knowledge or education were the only sooth-ing thing in the world, Van Loon was teaching—whispering in my ear, his eyes skewing right or left into the trees away from the scene in the clearing. "You see, it's supposed to be the moon," he told me about the circle of shouting hunters. "Each position has a meaning. That's why they were fighting about them. The guy in yellow slippers is at the moon's anus—seriously—*Tycho*—a place of honor. And those boys along what would be *Mare Imbrium*—prestigious—they're all Tarkonet . . . "

I tried to swallow panic and feigned an absurd interest. "If they're shooting in a circle—aren't there accidents?"

"There have been."

"This is insane."

"They aim low."

There was a shout. Van Loon fell to his knees, fussed with the hem of his blue robe and, I think, pretended to retie his boots. A volley of arrows made a noise like a hummingbird. Immediately a second volley, then several stray arrows.

Five arrows were lodged in the man's thighs and lower back or buttocks. One had driven downward through his forearm staking it firmly to the ground. The man stared at a blossom of red and yellow feathers jutting from his inner elbow. The worst wound—fatal before long—had been made by an arrow aimed high, which must have run straight through the man's neck before flying out of the circle of hunters. Strangely, when the circle started breaking up, the hunters seemed more interested in finding this prize arrow than in their prey. Two arrows had also pierced the bird, but it was still alive. The ends of the arrows kept getting stuck in weeds when it tried to move.

The dying man made no sound. His free hand squeezed the exit wound at his throat. He seemed unaware that dark blood jetted to the rhythm of his heart from a hole in the back of his neck. Although the clearing was full of relaxed activity now, no one spoke above a whisper. A hunter from somewhere below the *Mare Crisium* grabbed the red bird and broke its neck with a stirring motion. He looked down at the dying man and, for all I could tell, casually informed him about the hole in the back of his neck. The man's hand crept backward, but that freed a gout of blood to spill onto his chest. He grabbed his throat again with a small moan of surprise. His eyes were wide. No one else paid him any attention.

Van Loon was humming monotonously under his breath. Otherwise the silence was uncanny. The sound of the stream and of a mule blundering in the underbrush rose to consciousness. The intermittent patter of blood jetting from the dying man's neck sounded just as natural, ordinary, like the sound of branches cracking or of water running over stones.

I was careful not to betray the slightest emotion. Van Loon and I said nothing. Under a fold of his blue robe, he held my hand tightly the whole way back. I was grateful for it, because it got me thinking about him instead of wallowing in self-disgust or in that stranger emotion I'd felt before—a happy and black grimness that it hadn't been me shot full of arrows.

For a change, Van Loon was untalkative. I hoped the occasional extra squeeze of my hand did him some good. When he'd recovered enough to breathe steadily and stop humming, he met my gaze a few times. The look was flat, as it had been when he rested his hand on my knee the other day. I started thinking about this friendship. Was our connection all business? Clearly he'd needed me for strength today. And he'd said his disdain for Topher when we first docked in Alejandrina had been about me, not the boy. That was odd. I took Van Loon to be a public personality, the kind of man who lived in broad, intellectual strokes. I didn't get from him the focused, adhesive, achy attention I recognized as an attachment—or a love—worth pursuing. Obviously he felt things, but his feelings were indecipherable to me. I could go through the motions with him—I could squeeze his hand or hold still when he rested his hand on my knee. Apart from that, he seemed as lofty and remote as the clouds, almost unreal.

I FELT SICK that night, prey to the same restlessness as the night before. Or worse. I checked on my treasure. I opened the access panel and, imagining the rope slack, retied it. I smoked cigarette after cigarette. Ol's pannikin was filled with butts and a stinking mud of ash. I decided it wouldn't be so irresponsible to go across the street for a while. I kidded myself that this hour's proximity to my boxes, this obeisance to my shipper's money, meant I had plans and they were on track. The reasoning felt corrupt even as I accepted it.

At Society shop clerks in garden-party white aped glamour with gestures as broad as the tightly packed crowd allowed. I wondered whether the day's bombings, omens of chaos, hadn't injected extra energy into the night's carouse, at least for the time being. Even I felt susceptible to unthinking excitement.

I saw no one I recognized, until a huge smile pooled in front of me, the ex-waiter from Riverina. He wasn't working tonight, not dancing at any rate. One of his hands was continually occupied yanking up oversized, beltless jeans. The other held a drink with six straws. He was smashed. He was in some black, sleeveless, clingy, half-transparent material, but my gaze kept skidding down

it, across his scrawny abdomen, past the gaping waistband to a
flash of red—last night's work clothes. Maybe he'd never made it
home. Plucking the waistband so it hung invitingly slack for me,
he zoned out, sipped. After a moment I looked up. I wandered
around the empty halls of his eyes for a while. I got him a fresh
drink in a new glass.

We could only hear little pieces of our conversation. It didn't
really fit together. But that was better. I was doing something I'd
never done before—talking in the helpless way of people who
need to talk.

First I complained about "this company" that was hounding me,
thinking I knew something about their missing money. I doubt the
ex-waiter heard me, but he picked up happily on my bitter tone
of voice and muttered, "Fuckers, fucking fakers."

Then I told him about my business. How a fat, smug Dadi
Anton halfway across the world expected me to make a trading
profit in a backward country with no leadership, no rule of law
and widespread investment only in death.

"*I'm* a businessman," the ex-waiter boasted. "I have a friend
who's an exporter. He's going to buy me two cars, and I don't
even have to have sex with him. He doesn't care about that. He
just likes me around." A straw pulled a thread of saliva from the
corner of his slurring mouth. A kneeling telamon on a cube tuck-
ing bills into his socks cracked, "For your mind, I'm sure!" and the
ex-waiter eyed me coyly and said, "What mind, right?"

"*Two* cars?"

"Yeah, but he's an idiot. Actually, I'm leaving. I'm not sticking around to be . . ." He was going to make a joke about getting

raped but didn't. "I loathe these fakers! I loathe, loathe this place." He held his jeans up by leaning against the wall and fluffed his hair with both hands.

"Come out for air a minute," I said.

He came, grabbing someone's half-empty beer bottle from a table as he passed. I shepherded him carefully through the crowd. I was afraid of losing him, if only as a handy container for conversation.

We walked to the spot where Topher and I had stood to look across the harbor at the Mandarin "Temple," which looked even worse tonight. One of the aqua spots was shorting out. Oddly enough, it felt perfectly safe standing there, half an ear cocked to the heartbeat-like noise of distant shelling. Notions of chance made this particular spot feel untouchable. For something to say I repeated Topher's description of the temple. As I talked, the ex-waiter peeled bits of label from the beer bottle and rolled the damp foil into pellets. "It was a friend of mine told me all that," I said. "My friend Topher Ammidon Smith. You've probably met him."

The ex-waiter drew Topher's scar down his chest and raised his eyebrows: *that one?* When I nodded, he mumbled something and shrugged.

"What?"

"I said he's a little grungy is all. You're friends?"

"Yeah, he's a friend."

"Oh. Well. I thought he was a dumb oaf. But that's *moi*. Or what one hears." It was a kind of joke. He made a flowery gesture, mocking himself and Topher and me, generally.

What I did then had nothing to do with my suspecting he was

the one who'd thrown a rock at Topher. I slapped the ex-waiter's face with the silly formality of the insulted. I calculated the force of the blow in a rapid cascade of thought involving infinitesimal deliberations about how much harm I wanted to do and what effect it would have on him. His smile pooled, so I hit him again, much harder.

"I hate you," he muttered, his hand trembling as he flicked a pellet of beer label at my chest. But his eyes were lowered, and the smile was leaking back again. I hit him several more times, adding a few light punches to either shoulder. Finally, he raised his arms in weak defense, whispering, "Hey, hey, hey, hey . . ."

Strange to say, I sensed, or imagined, deliberations in his mind parallel to my own. His defense was weak in proportion to obscure consent in my attack. He was easy to topple on account of drunkenness. When he crawled a little ways, his jeans slid to his knees, the red underwear bunched. He held my boot lightly as I kicked him. It felt like he was drawing my foot toward him but he was subtly redirecting the blows from the soft spot above his hip to his ribcage. An elegant tortoiseshell fountain pen he'd pickpocketed earlier tipped from the folds of his pants. Before it could roll away, I stomped on it with my heel, shattering it.

My violence kept to a weird mathematics. I was still holding back, but as he was hurt more, I was allowed to do more harm. I'd seen it happen before with the Langlais brothers and Clancy Rasmussen. But this case was different, or I was different. My imaginary contract with the ex-waiter came nowhere near involving his death. Still, as he hugged my boot tighter I got enraged at what felt like his gauzy control over this whole beating. I stooped and hit his bloodied ear with the back of my hand. I hesitated, a little out of breath, exhilarated. The pleasure was undeniable.

The ex-waiter whimpered a few times. "You're scaring me," he whispered. He immediately vomited, the yellow fluid spilling from the side of his mouth and drawing skeins of blood from swollen lips. He choked several times.

"Faker!" was my initial black, ecstatic thought, horrible as it sounds. I crouched and helped him sit up.

"Stay away from me," he said shrilly, but his hands clung to mine. Acid burning in his sinuses, he sniffed and snorted tenderly. A globus of bloody mucus descended. His eyes crumpled shut under a web of tears that glimmered in viscous threads and scallops on his lashes and eyelids.

I helped him to his feet. Coming back to myself, I was full of worry, because at first he couldn't walk except half bent over, clutching the waistband of his jeans to his belly. The contract of violence—the way I imagined it anyway—made him my responsibility now. I helped him limp across the street. We said nothing to each other.

It was the second time I brought an injured boy to the Colebart. Tonight the place was locked. Through the barred glass, I could see the night clerk sleeping under a ratty blanket on the leather deco armchairs, which he'd pushed together. He got up resentfully but fast enough. I said something deliberately incoherent about an accident. Cued, the ex-waiter let out a few explanatory whimpers. I realized he'd been suppressing them, because he knew I didn't like the sound.

In the sixth-floor shower room I had the boy strip and looked

him over the best I could in the weak light. Vast bruises, like diffus-
ing blots of iodine covered his right side. His head was bloodied,
but I was most worried about his insides. I turned him and gently
pressed a bruise over one kidney. He moaned. I asked whether the
pain was on the inside or at the surface. "Surface."

I turned him around and pressed on his side and ribs. "Inside
or surface?"

"Surface . . . I think."

I checked on the dilation of his pupils just like I had with
Topher.

"Now I like you," he said drily when his pupils shrank a bit to
forty watts. "You're very considerate when you maim a guy for
life." Laughter was obviously painful, because he grimaced, and
tears sparked from the brinks of his cheeks and dripped to the
floor.

"Wash up," I said, draping one of the thin hotel towels over his
bony shoulder. To say I was sorry was by far inadequate. But I was
acting so severely, he probably never guessed how it felt to look
over my work. He may even have imagined I felt I had the insane,
natural righteousness of the Langlais brothers or ECOMILG thugs
or the Mandarins or terrorists. I didn't.

When he eased the door to my room open, I'd already rinsed
his shirt of vomit. I'd knocked the sludge from the pannikin and
was smoking at the window, rubbing a thumb over Ol's scratches
and swirling a puddle of fresh water until it was thick and black.
The boy looked a little better. He held himself straight, the towel
cinched very neatly around his waist.

"How do you feel?"

"Not so drunk. I'm angry at you." He dropped his gaze.

"I shouldn't have hurt you like that. Obviously." I was rubbing Ol's scratches like a chaplet.

The ex-waiter's smile appeared. He tried to hide it, directing it at the floor. At last he mastered it, and it seemed to fall from his mouth like a great drop of blood. He looked up at me.

"Sure you're OK? Nothing deep?" I asked.

"Luckily, I'm getting out of this dump of a city, so you won't be able to beat me up anymore." It was, believe it or not, a little coy, a little hopeful.

For a second I had a panicky sense of what absolute freedom would be like—not necessarily a good thing. It almost showed on my face as a certain kind of stare, a making-myself-at-home in his empty eyes. Instead, I asked offhandedly, "Leaving Alejandrina? How're you managing that?"

"I already got a job on the first ship going out," he said in the bragging voice I didn't trust. Bitterly, he added, "Probably fuck my brains out the whole way, but that'll be better than . . ."

"Which ship?"

He saw I doubted him and smiled. "*Narses*. It isn't posted yet."

"How'd you hear about it?"

"A friend."

"So, when's it going out?"

"They don't know yet."

"That means the cargo isn't full up?"

"I'm not sure. Nothing yet, I think."

"Crew?"

"The crimps'll get a crew at the last minute probably."

"They taking passengers?"

"Maybe." Brightening, he held his hand out for a cigarette. "You can't act! I knew you liked me. I could tell as soon as I saw you. And I'm not that bad, am I?" He spread his arms.

I smiled at him, but my thoughts were far away. I felt a strangely pleasurable disappointment realizing Van Loon had lied to me. He wasn't going to help me get out of the city. I'd have to do it myself.

9

ANDERS WILLIS FOUND me the next morning. The day clerk handed me a stack of polite messages from company representatives, which I stuffed in my pocket and forgot. I went to the waterfront. Passage on the *Narses* was easy to book. I did so at James Osbert and Co. in a clean office, signing papers in a way that seemed perfectly routine. They were happy to accommodate a small cargo. Unfortunately, no sailing date was set. When it was, the *Narses* would be posted as departing. Their house flag was a blazing sun in a black lozenge on white.

The one unusual circumstance was a demand for payment in cash. By the time two Osbert agents showed up at my hotel, a single blue box of silver (with a scratched lid) was out on my bed for them. I unpacked eight hundred silver dollars, which they stowed in a belted leather chest before heading off with guards who'd waited by the hotel entrance. The price was also unusual, unusual enough, I suppose, to take me and my boxes as far as the moon and back. It was going to be hard to recoup, and even harder to explain to Dadi Anton.

At least I now had a plan to get out, and it should have relieved me, but it didn't. I had time to think about all the unthinkable things I'd seen. I closed the shutters of my room against the intense sun but stood there with a cigarette peering through the slats. The sameness of always stationing myself there, pannikin in hand, was a tiny grace note of routine that calmed me in a way I can't describe. Even if I couldn't get to the lowest, most heavenly, state of existence, I could mimic it through perfect stillness. But the dull regularity couldn't quash thought. Unlike myself, I had flickers of revolted self-consciousness about my character. The perverse truth was that I found love almost too painful to bear, but violence and mistrust made such pleasurable good sense to me I luxuriated in them. I watched the tendrils of smoke feel their way through the slats into the dazzling heat of the sun outside, then reverse course and twine back into the room and sink. I wondered if this wasn't the perfect image of a freak eddy I was caught up in myself. A slow, expiring cycle, as slow as the backward-moving mandarins' celestial gyres, but even more charged with forgetfulness. I had to get out of the room.

An air of boredom and suspended activity hung over the docks, the intense boredom that fills empty moments when disasters are an everyday thing. When I walked through the harbor's maze of squared-off water and lapboarded godowns, I saw no one, but the water carried the whining voices of Chinese stokers crouched somewhere over a game of fan-tan. Though no one could find crews, the slips were crowded. A steam freighter rode high and cargoless, its motion-hungry bow plates weeping rust, while directly across the way at a place called Green's Yard tawny ziggurats of deal were already mold-streaked and likely to rot before anybody got them out of Alejandrina. Lighters and ships of every kind had anchored in a grid in the harbor, subtly rising and falling like loose rivets before a boiler explosion. Saddest of all was a docked Indiaman, mere ripples pattering against its glamorous cutwater.

Curious that the city wasn't busier, I went up Sufferance Street where most of the ministries were located. Even there crowds were less than in days past. I wondered whether people hadn't given up trying to leave before the insurrection swept downcountry. Anders Willis's headquarters happened to be on Sufferance Street, a modern glass building exuding thoughtless, first-world power. The looming police headquarters and Presidential Palace nearby, with their plumed guards and bereted thugs in pillboxes, projected power only too self-consciously. The way I paused under an arcade drew a lazy stare from one machine gunner.

I'd paused because I'd spotted Topher Ammidon Smith saying goodbye to Bill Sawtell on the Anders Willis steps. From the way they were standing I guessed they'd just been inside the building. The goodbye was long and unsmiling and ended with a hug. After Sawtell was out of sight, I caught up with Topher heading to the waterfront.

Topher dropped back into step with me and said with a hint of mockery, "You know I saw you there. I didn't tell Bill."

"I couldn't care less."

"He's not crazy about you right now."

"We're not cut out to be friends."

Not entirely friendly himself, Topher wondered, "I can't imagine you having a mother and father. I mean I can't imagine what you'd be like with them."

"Just like anybody," I said coldly. I told him I thought he was angry because I had to leave the city. I told him I'd booked passage, the whole thing was set. He shrugged. "Why so moody, then?" I asked.

"Problems," he said. Then he lied, or half lied. "It's just having to see my father. I get all . . . You ever have to deal with somebody who's crazy?" He looked at me and answered the question himself. "I guess not. Well, it's hard. He's nervous about bombs."

"You're pretty devoted considering what a bastard——"

Topher eyed me.

I sighed. "Everybody's afraid of bombs, right?"

He laughed a little harshly. "Yeah, like that fool at the Colebart when we showed up with all the boxes."

"Think he thought we were bombers?"

"Clock salesman?" he asked sarcastically. "Could've looked that way to him. Suspicious. Especially you come in with this lowlife covered with blood."

"I don't think you're a lowlife."

He stopped and addressed me gravely. "Wrong word. I meant it in a good sense. Like regular guy. Different from you. You're the type could be with whoever you wanted."

"Topher, let's sit and talk a minute."

He actually speeded up. "I don't feel like sitting. I got to get back to the boat. We might have this other job soon."

"What's that."

"Mm. Not sure yet."

"Hold on."

"What?" He frowned as if in the midst of reading a fog had come between him and the page. The expression lasted a long time.

I was able to talk him into going to Society in its guise as a cocoa room, but he relented sullenly and wouldn't talk much. He refused coffee, beer, everything. Since I wasn't having any luck talking to him about what mattered to me just then, I turned to the truly important business and sounded, if anything, more relaxed. "So what were you guys doing in there?"

I'd guessed right, but he said, "Where?"

"Anders Willis."

"Oh. Yeah, we were there, I guess. Him too. Sawtell."

"What was he up to?"

"I don't know," he lied. "He works for them. Maybe they had something they had to talk to him about. I don't really know."

"What about you, then? What were you doing?"

He pretended not to hear, then, like a child, folded his arms on the table and laid his head on them. His fragmenting blue eyes were alert but dissociated from anything in the shadowy room. He was clearly exhausted. In a few days he'd become deeply tanned, which made the down on his jaw stand out like frost. His savaged fingertips rhythmically made dimples in his upper arms. Even slack, the muscles were too massive for his age. "If I go with the captain, I might have to leave my dad here," he said.

"Is the captain taking the *Myrrha* someplace?"

"He's thinking of taking the boat down the coast for this buyer and then flying back to the US. His health isn't so good."

"He found someone who'll buy the boat?"

"Yeah, and he wants me to crew—or pilot. It would be good to get out." He sat up and looked more adult than I'd ever seen him. "It's really getting bad here. I'm worried about my dad, though. And what if this buyer won't keep me on the job? You're on the *Narses*? You were lucky to find something. I didn't know they were outbound. I didn't know anybody was."

"There's no date yet. It isn't posted."

"How'd you find out, then?"

"I beat up that kid who threw a rock at you. He told me."

For the first time that day Topher smiled, though it was a small smile. I think the notion of vengeance flattered him, a quality I didn't like. He shrugged, fell back on to the table and buried his smile in the crook of his elbow. He lifted his chin to say, "Not so impressive, though. Wimpy little Aussie faggot."

"So what were you doing there?"

"Where?"

"Anders Willis."

"No big deal. I lost my papers. Captain started freaking out about crimps and made me go. Anders Willis just helped get my papers back."

"They weren't asking anything about us?"

"Us?"

"Me and the captain, I mean."

"Anders Willis? What would they be asking me about you guys?"

"Because we were supposed to go talk to them about . . . "

"Oh, about what happened in B. I'm not sure. Maybe they did talk about it." He pretended to try and remember.

"Cut it out, Topher!" I said angrily. "Just tell me what they said."

"They said the whole crew up there was killed. Including Sawtell's brother."

"Which one was he?"

"Chris Sawtell."

"That was the one they sent for water," I murmured.

Accusingly, he said, "You might want to talk to Bill some time about being the last guy to see his brother alive, instead of keeping everything to yourself. Though I don't know if he wants to talk to you. I don't think he likes you much. He's little, but he could probably take you."

"What else did they talk about?"

"Just that!" he shouted. "Those guys are dead! You care anything about it?" Newspapers rustled and old men cleared their throats in the silence. Someone stirred sugar into his coffee. More calmly Topher said, "They didn't ask me anything about you." He was lying.

"Surprising," I said. "Nice of them to get your papers for you, though. And I wonder who's buying the *Myrrha*? I bet one of the companies could get it away from the government and send it down the coast. Maybe keep the old crew on as a favor to the captain. I guess that would make you an employee of Anders Willis just like Sawtell. If it happened, I mean."

Topher was getting offended by my tone.

I went on. "They probably should talk to you, if you're going to work for them. A nice long interview. Get all your impressions about what happened in B."

"Yeah, and maybe I'd tell them how kind of sleazy you acted," he said angrily.

I waited.

"You know what I mean. You left too soon!"

"You think we left too soon?"

"Come on! It's exactly the same thing—I don't know if I should leave my dad behind. Maybe not exactly the same."

"What did I have to do with the *Myrrha* leaving?" I said quietly. It wasn't self-righteous rhetoric. In a way I was asking myself. I could see that Topher, who thought he already knew what had happened, read something else into my wan question, a kind of weaselly admission. I'm not sure why I decided to let the impression stand. Maybe it was easier to be hated.

I know that as I looked over him—and we were seated very close—I didn't love him. Not at that moment. It had nothing to do with his visit to Anders Willis or his anger at me. It was more like a storm clearing, the mood of my heart changing, my level of existence shifting. It could have been that Van Loon or the violence with the ex-waiter had interfered with my state of mind. But not loving Topher was as powerful an emotion as loving him. Somehow it involved giving up forever the possibility of touching him. I can't describe how much this particular aspect of eternity hurt with the skin of his shoulder right there, inches from my lips. He may have felt the same despair, that he could never have me—not my skin, in his case, but *me*. I don't know whether he did. It's almost impossible to know what another person is feeling.

"Don't worry about it," Topher said finally. He almost touched me, and I looked around nervously at the old men, all of them stuck again in pharaonic immobility. Topher sighed. "I lied just then. I talked to them. They asked what happened. I had to talk a little bit to get my papers. I told them about the guy they killed next door. I told them it was all confused. They think I'm a stupid kid."

"There *is* nothing to tell, though, is there?"

He shrugged.

"There's nothing to tell."

"I don't betray . . . I don't betray anybody."

"Look, we trust each other. We're friends. I don't think there's anything to tell. There's nothing to tell." I was starting to sound machine-like, vaguely hysterical.

For the first time ever Topher looked at me with real concern.

I said, "The truth is there's nothing to tell. I know you think I somehow told the captain to go. Are you saying they think that, too, now?"

"It's not me you have to worry about," Topher said earnestly. "Captain's been talking to Anders Willis all along. He's the one told them about your stuff. I had to say, 'Yeah, there were boxes.'"

"And my hotel."

"Yeah, and where you were, but they would have found out. I was pissed off about you going with the Mandarins."

"Did you tell them I had money in the boxes?"

"I told them I didn't know what was in them. The captain told them it was coin. He guessed."

"So they think I have their gold. Or part of it."

He looked at me, curious about that himself. When I didn't

answer—I had too much to think about—he blew a sigh, making a tight ring of his mouth, which almost made a flaxen mustache condense on his upper lip. "I'm so tired!"

THE ELEVATOR OPENED on every floor of the Anders Willis building. Each time I glimpsed disarray, young men in suits dropping stacks of papers and files into bankers' boxes. Only on the top floor did anyone seem to be doing ordinary work. The suave company lawyer escorting me said everyone there was investigating events in B.

Government overseers sat at desks along one wall, but vacant desktops and idleness made it obvious they were being treated as contemptible rubber stamps. I saw several Mandarins, as well. Their oligarchy-in-exile had its own huge building on Sufferance Street, but I'd learned from Van Loon that Anders Willis was cunningly asking them to participate in all sorts of projects, then trying to keep their representatives immobilized by scrupulous protocol.

I waited in a glass pen and pretended to watch the activity on the office floor. There was something "courtroom" about the setup, which made me a little panicky. Waiting with me were an older gentleman in a suit and a sissified young man, perhaps his son, who wore an orchid T-shirt, white jeans and black loafers. The son had been crying. The father ignored him manfully. The young man rummaged through a monogrammed canvas beach bag. He took out a new package of aspirin (which looked like it had been bought in the United States), ripped at it and got the bottle out.

He pulled the squeaky cotton from the throat of the bottle and kneaded it into a pad. Sniffling as he bent forward, he slipped the pad into his loafer and pressed a raw heel home after it.

The lawyer returned from another room, motioning me to follow. As soon as he shut a glass door, he said discreetly, "Those two are—here—" We shuffled farther from the door. "As you can imagine we've asked everyone with an interest in Bottom hong—"

I already had a feeling everything I said would be out-of-true. Facing questions was more daunting than I'd expected. I'd always pitied the chumps browbeaten into confessing crimes they didn't commit, convinced I'd be the ultimate cool customer in their shoes. But now I was afraid to talk. Nothing I could say was going to come out sounding either logical or believable. Worse, I might "confess." Stonewalling—total ignorance—felt like the only safe course. So I asked, "Bottom hong?"

"Bottom hong. Our hong in B. Where you stayed. You didn't even know the name?" He gave me a friendly smile.

"No. Bottom hong. Funny, I didn't."

"Well, anyway, those two are the Havers. Father and brother." He didn't look at them through the glass. "We brought them from the U.S. before the bombings got so bad. Felt like we owed them that, though now that things have gotten . . . They're the family of our young Mr. Haver, who was in charge at Bottom. Disappeared or killed, I'm afraid. I'm sure they'd appreciate it, if you remembered anything particular . . ."

I looked through the glass. Such an unlikely and disoriented pair. Thought of the cotton wad set up an astringent reaction in my mouth. "Haver. I'm sure I must have met him, but . . . I don't remember."

"It was only on the chance you did," the lawyer shrugged. His confident mildness unnerved me.

There were several people in the conference room, but my eyes were drawn to the table. The surface was polished to an intense sheen like a chasm. Files seemed to skid or float on upwelling, dark, glazed air. Maybe it was weak of me to notice, but the illusion of bottomlessness had an arresting, almost suicidal, beauty.

On one side was the captain, who didn't look at me. I nodded in his direction anyway. They'd provided him an extra large mahogany armchair, which, even so, compressed his sides and pushed them up. In his clean olive uniform shirt he looked like a monstrous bud, calyces curling open. A yellow ascot peeked from under the fleshy sheath of his neck like a tightly folded petal just showing. The captain seemed to doze or hide, his eyes almost closed. Two government officials—observers? overseers?—sat against the wall behind him. Across the table were two Anders Willis men, old and young. The suave lawyer joined them. I sat at the end of the table.

Papers, pens and water glasses made me think they'd been talking for some time. I was wary of what might be unfair friendliness toward the captain. Maybe our status wasn't equal, but in a neutral investigation he shouldn't be sitting in while I answered questions. I didn't want to make a guilty-seeming fuss, so I didn't protest. The country was all but at war, not the time to be a stickler. Instead, I said to the older Anders Willis man, who was presiding, "You must be the captain's cousin." I had to know immediately, if that was the case.

The captain woke promptly. "You misremember." "That was the *old* captain, my friend, whose cousin works here. But he's not *here*, of course."

The captain's "of course" made it sound like the investigation had formal proprieties. In that context, the word "misremember" put me at a disadvantage right from the start. "I meant the old captain," I said, my thoughts racing.

The Anders Willis men smiled benignly. They asked me to sketch the fall of the hong as I'd observed it. My report was too brief and vague for them. They led me through my stay day by day, the last day hour by hour. The details made my claim not to remember Haver sound implausible. I announced this myself. I acted as if my memories had a prodigious lightness, appearing and rising, full of their own curious will to be described. And in fact, the step-by-step method did bring back a lot I'd forgotten. I had to outrace the memories, choosing, rejecting. Any faster and my thinking might have blurred into that dizzying cascade of calculation that had come when I attacked the ex-waiter. And who could I attack here? It was impossible to stonewall. I'd come off a monster. I stumbled a few times. I talked too much. I admitted knowing tea caddies, dresses, sugar, pepper had been in the godown. Not gold, of course.

Now their questions jumped from moment to moment of the last day. Didn't I remember seeing Haver at such-and-such a time? It felt like they were trying to trip me up.

"Clearly," I said, "I must have seen him several times. I'm sure

I talked to him, too. The problem is I just don't remember. You have to understand each of us was completely preoccupied with his own . . . business."

"I asked him about Haver myself," the lawyer put in. He turned to me, friendly but not warm. "His brother says he had a linen suit. Also an ordinary gray business suit." His photograph floated across the chasm to me.

Why deny Haver? flickered through my mind. Why deny him when it was dangerous and pointless? I had no time to answer myself. "Of course, yes, I remember him now. I saw him several times. But I don't remember any—any specific interactions. I don't think I saw him the last day."

The youngest Anders Willis man gave me a look full of doubt and dislike. His expression made my heart race. The polite sham of the meeting seemed about to evaporate. He demanded, "How can you have known—and pretty accurately—almost everything that was in the godown? Who told you?"

"I think I had a discussion—not with Haver—about putting my own things in the godown, which I thought might be safer. The city was unsettled already. And this person—was it the one called Kurball? Burly?—he told me the godown was full of dresses, tea caddies, sugar, whatever I said. Only after I read the papers here did it occur to me, maybe . . ."

"Gold?"

"Kirbie?"

"Kirbie. That's right," I said.

"And your 'things'? That would be the boxes, I assume. They contained . . . ?"

I didn't answer. I was so attached to the secret. I turned to the government officials. "Should I be represented? I'm sure the captain filed a manifest with the harbormaster or whoever has authority for the port in Alejandrina. Would that be public? Do I have to answer someone who—well, evidently, someone who's a potential competitor?"

I was bullshitting and got exactly what I deserved. One of the government officials wagged his whole upper body back and forth to convey the incredible difficulty of the question and gibbered to the floor, "In some cases, yes. In some cases, no. There are circumstances when a duty assessment is challenged—outbound *or* inbound, mind you—or whenever litigation . . ."

"I filed a standard manifest, of course," the captain broke in. "What did I know but that he had boxes? There wasn't any inspection. Understand, it was a terrible moment. I could see blue boxes with my own eyes. That was enough. I had no idea what was in them and still don't."

"Or if one is talking about contraband, a very great problem," the government official added pointlessly.

"It's been said the blue boxes contained coin," the captain ventured.

"Silver." I shrugged.

The young Anders Willis man laughed. "Ah. It had that ring to you, captain? Silver, not gold?"

The captain turned the rings on one hand and modeled them for himself. "Size and weight. It was my guess they had coin. That's all."

The lawyer said, "Let's calm down. Let's not get . . . I think things will go more smoothly if we keep in mind our purpose is as much humanitarian as it is . . . Try to remember the Havers and Mr. Bustamante and Mr. Sawtell and all the others we've talked to . . ."

For some reason, this remark came off as the most threatening thing I'd heard that day. I decided to change tack—a mistake, maybe—and quietly admitted, "They did tell me about the gold." The young one struck the chasm with a pen. "My dog kept chasing a pair of cats they had, ratters, and the cats would hole up in the godown. So—Kirbie I guess his name is—and I would go in to flush them out. I could see for myself what was in the godown. Tea caddies wrapped in cardboard and newspaper, china, the commodities, exactly what I said, what I'd been told. I was surprised to see they had so much stuff on hand, and I told him it was crazy. And he told me, 'That's nothing. We've got two hundred big ones in gold in the strong room here and back in there.'"

"'Back in there' meaning in the hong?"

"Yeah."

"Where in the hong?"

"I never knew. Not in the big room upstairs. Anyway, I thought he was bragging. It followed from the way he and I didn't quite get along. He thought I was looking down my nose at them. He kept making a big stink about being a trained medic. He thought that was impressive."

"And you're sure 'big ones' are thousands?" the young guy demanded, pure hostility.

No one said anything, until the old man grumbled slowly, "Have you told your friend Mr. Van Loon what you're telling us now? Now that you *have* told us something."

"As a matter of fact I didn't. I mentioned the stuff they had in the godown, but I never told him about the gold. I don't think I trusted him."

"But you trust us."

"I'm afraid of you. I need to get out of the city."

The lawyer broke the faint, escalating tension. "I'm curious to know why you killed the dogs." He was referring to notes he'd written during my account.

"All the pets," I corrected. "It was such a bad moment. As the captain said. A few days before, we'd broken open a Lutheran medical cargo—for veterinary supplies, because it looked like the animals, the dogs, needed worming."

"They lost weight?" the young one barked. I didn't mind his swaggering and foolish questions, but the lawyer and the "boss" looked like they were getting impatient.

I said, "No. One of the guys—not Haver, not Kirbie—had a dog, too, and his dog kept going down to a strip of grass by the wall to Cricket hong—where, incidentally, the insurrectionists could've broken in at the end—and he dragged himself on it, rubbing his ass on the grass. You've seen it, I'm sure. It means they have worms. My dog started doing it, too. But this is all beside the point. We had the medical cargo open already—"

The young one broke in. "You know, my dog had worms, and he never did that."

I smiled at the lawyer. He didn't smile back. They wanted to present a united front. I waited a while to let the irrelevance of the question sink in. Then I answered precisely. "These were pinworms. They lay their eggs around the asshole, and it causes itching."

Gently, the lawyer murmured to his colleague, "OK, OK. Let's keep on track. So you had medical supplies ready . . ."

"I was only suggesting it could have gotten us going. Having the cargo open may have sparked the train of thought, which I admit was strange. This was the night before the *Myrrha* arrived. We thought we were going to be besieged for a while, and the pets would be a hindrance or unsanitary."

"You're claiming no one ever mentioned the rule?" the young one asked belligerently.

"What rule?"

The lawyer explained. "There's a company rule. Employees can't transfer livestock from upcountry. It's a matter of disease control. Some nasty diseases are endemic around B. Of course, as a guest, as a passenger, you would have been exempt. Your dog could have come. Put into quarantine here in Alejandrina a few days. But that's all."

"I didn't know."

"Fuck," the young one spat out.

The lawyer headed off an outburst. "It's a touchy subject. You see, our employee, Bill Sawtell, says his brother Chris had a dog, so you would have been dealing with him at that point. Some of us knew him."

"No one ever mentioned the rule."

"You don't get it," the young one couldn't contain himself. "If they were killing all the animals, then the crew definitely planned to leave B with the captain."

"I see they must have."

"How'd you do it?"

"Carbon monoxide in a pet crate. Then we injected them with sodium pentobarbitol. From the medical cargo."

"Why did you even bring your dog into the country?"

It was the hardest question they'd asked. My mouth hung open and my mind was a dazzling blank. Why had I brought him? It had just been my—desire. I didn't know how that was expressed. The sound of seven men breathing in the room got so loud I finally managed, "I had no one to leave him with."

"OK," the lawyer continued. "Your boxes were in the upper room of the hong. You got them all onto the *Myrrha*. Nothing got on from the godown, which was much closer. Why do you think that was?"

"All I can say is foresight on my part. They must have been slow organizing. Preoccupied with the siege, too, obviously."

"Were you helping in the defense?"

Instead of answering, I played what I thought was my only card. "As a matter of fact one box did get on from the godown. I saw a box covered with Anders Willis labels." Turning to the captain, I said, "You remember. You had it with you in the wheelhouse."

Without looking at me the captain fluttered his rings over the abyss, explaining casually, "The one I mentioned."

Though the Anders Willis men nodded and seemed satisfied, I tried, "I never saw what was inside it. Or did you say papers and—was it gold coins?"

"Silver," the captain croaked.

I'd been holding off on the key issue. That the captain left B early on his own initiative. It would be his word against mine, and I didn't know how best to make my case. I figured if I asked him aggressive or mocking questions, I'd sound unreliable. Now I felt cornered. Impetuously, but in the mildest voice I could manage, I asked him, "Why didn't you wait?"

I was stunned by the lack of reaction. The captain said nothing. He may even have shrugged imperceptibly. The lawyer and the old man were silent as well. Their expressions made me think I'd raised an issue they didn't want to deal with.

Only the young Anders Willis man responded. He hit the table, leaned across it, fixed *me* with a hateful stare and said, "*Fuck, yes! Why?*"

The "boss" stopped things. Ominously, he said, "Let's keep our eye on the gold, please." As an afterthought, he added, "For the time being." Standing up, he addressed me politely. "I hope you'll excuse us for being a bit overwhelmed at the moment. We must sound confused. I want to do a quick review of our questions, if you don't mind. It won't take long." He led the other two out of the room. They left so quickly the lawyer had to double back to grab several confidential files from the abyss.

Now that it didn't count, my tongue got looser. I asked the captain, "Why didn't you let Topher go back for the men? He asked you."

The captain shifted uncomfortably in his chair, his body some-how hinting it would be indiscreet for us to talk with the two government officials sitting there. I didn't care. When I opened my mouth to ask again, the captain said, "It was—it was a turbulent moment, to say the least. Dangerous."

"Topher's a brave kid. He would have been in and out. They might have listened to him. Maybe in a way they wouldn't have with you or me. Why not try?"

He mumbled something.

"What?"

Crossly he said, "Gunfire. I said, 'gunfire.'" He tried turning in his chair but couldn't manage it. He spoke over his shoulder to the government officials. "This is not, my conversation with this man is not, I believe, part of the—uh—official record. But before I go on I'd like to know, has the government given Anders Willis a letter of intent to sell the *Myrrha*?"

The two officials looked at each other uncomprehendingly.

The captain, who couldn't turn far enough to see them, demanded, "Well, has it?"

"I don't think they know anything," I said. "So why'd you leave B?"

"It was dangerous."

"It turned out to be. For the crew."

"It was dangerous," he repeated tightly.

"Why didn't you warn them?"

Until this moment the captain had been letting a pencil drop repeatedly into the chasm. And each time a reflected pencil rose and stopped it, eraser to eraser. Now he blew up. The pencil skated across the table. "Shut up!" he shouted. His wrists came down on the table edge, their fresh green cuffs as big as collars. "I would never send someone I cared about running across a yard with bullets flying! Maybe you can do that. Not me." He had tears of—I think—rage in his eyes. "I suppose I'm not such a tough-minded man as you, Mr.—*Vampire!*"

Before his rage could sink in—and what I imagined I was really seeing was love, raw and completely unexpected—the suave lawyer returned alone. Anders Willis had decided on a straightforward tactic. They wanted to inspect my belongings to see whether I had silver enough to fill the boxes I was known to have brought out of B. A government official would conduct the search as a duty inspection. Though I was preoccupied by the captain's outburst, I had the presence of mind to point out that the timing was inappropriate and that, in theory, no inspection should be carried out with Anders Willis representatives present.

The lawyer shrugged. "Why don't you relax? Clear it with your shippers. We'll speak to them as well."

"You don't know who my shippers are. No one does."

"Sorry, but we do. Within the past two days, Mr. Dadi Anton has been in touch with us at least three times. As a matter of fact, he was asking *us* to find *you.*"

I flushed, then got cold. It was possible. I'd been out of touch for quite a while. If I asked the lawyer any questions, I'd look foolish, even renegade. What kind of person doesn't know what his own employers are up to? What kind of employee lights out?

My expression must have been plain enough, because the lawyer answered me. "We do know him. It was on his account you were invited to stay at Bottom hong in the first place."

I waved that information away, pretending it was old news.

"Well, if you've been speaking to him, he must have confirmed what I just told you. I have *silver*. I don't have any of your gold."

"What he said was that *when you left Z* you had silver. And that you've been out of touch with him for a long time."

I was told to wait for inspectors at my hotel the following day.

10

GOING BY THE SOUND of things—remote explosions and all-night whispering up and down the Colebart halls—the situation in the city degenerated during the night. No newspaper came out the next morning. I'd run out of cash and expected to need more for bribes soon. I took twenty dollars from the box with a scratched lid, which left only $688. I was afraid the void was big enough the Anders Willis inspectors would think I'd had gold in that box. But I had the Osbert receipt for passage on the *Narses*—$800.

I was overwhelmingly tired. I laid some of the coins in a rosette on the bedside table, alternating heads and tails in a neat pattern. Like many misers I was absorbed by figures. They calmed me. Of course, I kept a running tally of the treasure in my head and

worried it with hypothetical expenses and gains. But my numeri-
cal intimacy with the treasure was deeper than that. I knew the
dimensions of the boxes. Each full box contained 1,500 coins in
stacks of thirty arranged on a 5x10 grid. Simple numbers, child's
play, really. But I also had a numismatic understanding of the coins
themselves. Their composition (.900 silver, .100 copper), their
dimensions (diameter 1.5 inches, thickness .125 inches), their
weight (420 grains, that is, 27.22 grams or .84 ounces).

Weight was the key to value. I knew there was no way every coin
could weigh exactly 420 grains. With all the moving and clucking, atoms were constantly shed from the reeded edges, or too
many atoms had been dosed in the eleventh or thirteenth grain.
(My absurd fantasy was that the coins had been created grain by
grain in sequence. There could be no more simple and true pro-
cess. One plus one plus one and so on, just as all of mathematics
is laboriously built by the father of numbers, Time.) But none of
the coins weighed exactly the same. Each had its own weight. In
fact probability dictated that each coin weighed a different and
irrational number of ounces. Not one of them could be weighed
precisely to the last decimal place. So every one of the coins had a
unique value that made a mockery of the raised letters ONE DOL-
LAR. They were supposed to be identical, but it was impossible
for me not to desire one more than another sometimes, if only in
theory. Idly, I rearranged the coins, obverses and reverses. When
ash from the cigarette between my lips fell on the design, I blew
it away with smoky breath.

It wasn't surprising Dadi Anton caught up with me that day. I
was on my way to the cocoa room, when the day clerk called me

back, nodding toward a teak phone nook next to the front desk. "For you. A Mr. Dadi Anton calling from Z." I told him to hold the caller while I got some papers. I ran up and down six flights simply to plan out what I'd say. I came back with pens and notebook, but they were useless props.

"Golly, you've been hard to reach," Dadi Anton said with almost foolish-sounding bonhomie, his usual false front.

"You've left messages at the hotel?"

"I meant it was hard to find your hotel. You forgot to leave us the name of the place. My assistant had to try a whole bunch of them. Then we got word. Tom Langlais and I know a couple of guys with an outfit down there."

"You're in Z? I thought you might be traveling."

"You're way out of date. I've already been and come back. Nice to be back. It's pretty here this time of year. Not like down there, huh?"

"You mean the—uh—political weather."

"Heh-heh, that's right. Very good. Very good!" After a pause he laughed again. He seemed to be thinking, feeling me out. There was also, I believed, an unusual hint of actual humor in the sound of his laughter, not necessarily a good sign. I'd always acted fearless around him, which men kippered by power sometimes appreciate. This time I wondered if the laugh didn't mean he was exploring a subtly different friendliness. Very dangerous if the need for deception were suddenly less. If it was valedictory friendliness.

I said, "As a matter of fact, I've just finished writing you a report about the situation here and in B and about my plans. Unfortunately, the phones are pretty much impossible down here. But now that we've got each other, let's not waste time explaining." My toes curled with the struggle to sound offhand, relaxed. I described what had happened in B, the short version.

"My gosh! My gosh! You've had a time of it, haven't you?" The extreme falsity of his exclamation soothed me. It jibed with my deepest sense of self. Obvious lies could never weigh you down with doubts the way earnestness did. "Now, have you run into any more problems in Alejandrina?" Dadi Anton cooed.

"No," I said too quickly. "Smooth sailing," I added in a jokey drawl. "I've booked out on a ship called the *Narses*. Unfortunately, the *Clay* left before I could rejoin her."

"Heard about that," he said commiseratingly. "They had to go straight out without stopping just to hang on to the crew."

"But with the *Narses*, like I said—smooth sailing. A tiny delay is all. They don't have a firm departure date yet."

"I see," he said neutrally. He sounded pained. "Mm. Delays can cause problems. Silly bookkeepers, right?" He went on thoughtfully, "What about . . . what about, when you do get out, coming back to Z to take stock?" He didn't sound quite firm on the idea. It would be the end of me.

"Mm," I echoed. "That would be a problem. I've already got a lot invested in—stuff I found particularly cheap on account of the political situation."

"I thought you said you were still liquid."

"No, I only meant 'in general.' Not the whole amount."

"No problem with export licenses and crap with things so . . ."

"Jeez, the other guys were talking about bombs!"

"People get spooked. It's not that bad."

"Could I ask what you've picked up?"

"Of course. It's nothing flashy, just solid, profitable stuff."

I sounded unconvincing. He murmured encouragingly for me to go on. As long as there was vagueness I felt I had a little power. But now our interests were lining up against each other. Needless to say my mind was racing. I hadn't even visited the export market yet. But the other night, when I doubted the ex-waiter's friend was going to buy him *two* cars, the kid had shrieked that his exporter was real. On backward-flexing fingers he'd ticked off exactly what his sugar daddy dealt in. "Well, some tulip nuts, first of all," I told Dadi Anton. "They're a local thing. Hulled, roasted and salted—I also got unsalted—they're kind of buttery like pignoli nuts."

"So those would be pine nuts?"

"I guess so. They're a lot bigger than you're used to, though. More like a cheap macadamia nut. Really very good. And they come in this amazing can with monkeys, and a river in a jungle and a radio tower. It's got a lot of exotic appeal, cult item material. And already passed for import into the U.S. and Europe." Coming out of a wave of faintness, I realized I was hunched over on a teak stool as if prepared for an explosion. The notebook was pressed to my lap. As I talked, I drew towers of diminishing boxes. I'd already created a dense, windowless city.

"What about reorders? If it flies."

"I've got a good relationship with the guy here. Totally reliable."

"If he manages to stay alive. Not to mention his business."

"I don't know what they've been telling you. Things just aren't as dramatic as all that. Never are, are they? More's the pity sometimes. But anyway, I also got these—these kind of rush tiles with adhesive backs. Great for home redecorating kicks and things like that. I know it sounds a little tired out or tacky, but I have a hunch these are going to work."

"What about bugs?"

"What do you mean?"

"People are going to think bugs'll get into the grass or whatever. You know, and dirt. Sounds dirty."

"Well . . ."

"It sounds dirty to me."

"No, no. They've got a very fine weave. Also this grass could be a natural repellent. I mean, we could say that. I could have little stickers printed up and slapped on: 'Alejandrina River Grass—a natural insect repellent.'"

"Come off it," he snorted. "So that's it?"

"Yeah." The line simmered. No, it was the sound of the blood in my ears, a sound like distant godowns on fire, the flames fanned by wind. I couldn't stand it. "Listen. I want to be straight with you. You sound sort of unimpressed. I don't think it's out of place for me to—remember, I was supposed to have a free hand. You always said, 'more than just a supercargo.' You've got to trust my instincts."

"All our guys have a free hand. Situation's different when a war breaks out—"

"No, that's completely—who are you talking to?"

"And what's this shit about gold? Sounds like you might have pissed some people off."

"That's completely untrue. The gold—I—"

"I'm not going to argue it. I'm not too worried you'll get yourself, or us, in real trouble. I don't see that happening, do you? Just suck up to them and get the hell out of there, OK?"

"That's exactly what I am doing. It wasn't worth crowing to you about it. I'm perfectly able to handle this."

"Yeah, well, I'd like you to come back to Z anyway, for a bit."

"I can't do that. I've already got the cargo set up with the *Narses*."

"Where's she going? No, it doesn't matter. Book it through to Z, New York, wherever. How much of the total was it?"

"I'm not sure. A lot. I've got my—I've been using office space on Sufferance Street during the day, and all my papers are there." Their very fluency made my lies seem too weak to stop him.

"Like I said, you book the cargo through to one of our importers wherever. As soon as you get to a big airport, fly straight back to Z with whatever's left of the silver. We'll regroup."

"No, I really can't do that. I've arranged to pack up the cargo, so the rush tiles don't show on the manifest. They're 'packing material.' It's a little fiddle, but it'll keep the apparent value down, so bribes will be lower all along the way. But I have to shepherd it through myself."

"Don't worry about that. Do up a complete manifest, put it through to wherever and come back here."

We paused. I felt like one of those hypnotizing, static volutes of water in a fast-running stream. It ought to dissolve, but it stays there.

Dadi Anton said crisply. "Look, it's our money, and we decide what happens to it, pal. It's very simple." He hung up.

AFTER THAT I must have gone off the rails for a while. What I planned was crazy, out-of-true, to say the least. My panting idea was to make all my lies true after the fact. I'd buy the rush tiles and the tulip nuts. But I'd buy a lot more, as well, spend almost the entire treasure. Then I'd call Dadi Anton and tell him I'd forgotten a few things—after all, the whole treasure was committed, and it couldn't be shipped through to just one importer, because the goods were selected for different markets. I'd have to travel with some of them.

In order to find the tulip nuts and the rush tiles, I needed to find the ex-waiter's fond exporter friend, if the man even existed. I decided to go down to the *Narses'* slip to see if the ex-waiter was there or where I could find him. I abandoned my pens and scribbled-on notebook right where they were.

As soon I left the phone nook, the day clerk stopped me. "Sir! Sir! While you were speaking . . ." He handed me a note I knew would be from the Anders Willis people. They were going to delay me with their absurd inspection just when I had to get out of the hotel.

Only it wasn't from them. It was too long and confusing to absorb at once. My head shot up. "Who brought this? Why didn't you tell me?"

"Sir! You were occupied. It was a boy."

The boy was only a messenger. The note was from Van Loon. Apparently he hadn't forgotten about me.

Turns out the Narses *will be the first to leave. Unfortunately, it's already been posted, but they're giving me the captain's saloon and I've made sure there's room for you. Hurry, though! It's scheduled to leave tomorrow. Book at James Osbert. Use my name, because the Mandarins are getting a last cargo out and I've been named their*

*supercargo. I have pull. Go to James Osbert's main office. Do not
come directly to the ship to book. She won't be there. Today we have
a skeleton crew doing sailing exercises. They're afraid we're top-
heavy with the cargo loaded. Van Loon.*

I was so agitated I decided to go to the waterfront whether the
Narses was there or not. Needless to say, I'd already booked passage, so that wasn't the problem. It was my fixed, deluded idea to
buy a big cargo of my own, and now I was worried there wouldn't
be room on the ship. I wanted to see the *Narses* with my own eyes.
And I was still hoping to find the ex-waiter. I knew I shouldn't
leave before the inspection of my boxes, but my invented responsibility was more important than the real one. Or that's how I
reasoned in a flash of anger.

It was the first time I'd been outside that day. After last night,
the atmosphere was tense. The cocoa room was open, but they'd
left their gray shutters lowered. Only a handful of people on anxious errands showed their faces on the streets. The *Narses'* berth
was in a densely packed section of the port (where the bowsprit of
that Indiaman had punctured a flophouse window when she first
attempted to dock). I almost got lost under the weave of masts
and rigging. Everything seemed still, until a movement came like
a lens drifting across the eye. Part of this jumble of structures was
afloat. A cool, narrow chasm between hull and dock—the sea—
was actually hard to find at first. Where the *Narses* was supposed
to be, white light snaked on open, greasy water.

Almost no one was around. Fishing equipment, traps and rolls
of net aged by the ocean, which were still used every night, looked

like they hadn't been touched in years and were strewn around in full decay. I wasn't sure the fishermen would come back for them tonight. Most sailors were probably in hiding, betting they were better off under the insurrection than on a ship. Two men I did spot at work looked like idiots. One chomped with fleshy lips as he scrubbed gull droppings from a huge davit—too gigantic, really, for the simple principle of fastening involved. It looked like something out of a fairy tale. The other man, for all I could tell, was counting the grommets of folded sailcloth in a tar-papered bin. I asked him about the *Narses*, and he pointed to Osbert's dockside office, a corrugated box on stilts with squinting ship-like windows and a queasy stairway around its spindly legs.

I found the ex-waiter fast asleep on a couch inside. From the office window he pointed out the *Narses* to me. She lay beyond the grid of ships anchored in the harbor. A pair of boats, maybe crimps' boats, nuzzled against the hull like kittens. Her sails were brailed up, so she may have had a practice run already. I could see why they needed to try her out. The holds must have been full, and the decks and superstructure were piled high with deal from Green's Yard. I'd never seen such an ungainly looking ship. The ex-waiter didn't know what time the *Narses* would be back. Though he gave me the address, he refused absolutely to take me to his exporter friend.

"I don't care if you think I'm a bullshitter," he whined. He tried to work up a fury, but he stared at the floor and couldn't help cringing his shoulders a bit. "What if none of this works out, and I need a friend here later? I don't want to go back and him be thinking, 'Oh, yeah, you're that flighty kid who came in hanging all over the crazy supercargo! Fuck you!' So fuck you! You are crazy if you want to go on some buying binge right when they're about to invade."

WHOLESALERS WERE AT one end of Alejandrina's main commercial avenue, a souk-like street of trinket-sellers, jewelers and electronics shops. Strips of red canvas yawned like gills when a breeze kicked up. The wind made me think of the *Narses* out in the harbor. I didn't want to be far from her for long. Most of the shops, all of the jewelers, were closed. But in the striped glare token displays of goods were laid out on scraps of cloth here and there, and merchants too attached to routine crouched, half in sunlight, half in shadow, discussing politics and war.

At first he was only a blinding nose, mustache and belly. Then the wind rose and sunlight eased back to show an acne-scarred face full of suspicion. His tubby shoulders were bare and frizzed with black hair. He'd torn the sleeves off his yellow "America College #1 Team" sweatshirt. I almost shook my head in wonder that the guy was real. But he didn't look like he could afford to give cars away.

I heard the first distant shelling of the day. The exporter shrugged at the sound, smiled ironically and led me into his shop. "Not many people open," I commented. He shrugged again, smiling as if to say, "What else can I do?" The man's eyes examined me carefully, not at all sure about someone who would shop today and sweated nervously. Nevertheless, he went through the motions. Behind the closed steel shutters and the dingy plate glass were,

surprisingly, walls of gorgeous slanted mahogany cubbyholes.
Each displayed a single bolt of brilliantly colored Madras. The shop
obviously dated back to the heyday of the Colebart, a time when
Alejandrina had been prosperous. The exporter showed me hack-
neyed brass salvers, silk flowers, and Fatima's hand ashtrays. He
laid out examples of L'Addresse Book in green, maroon, black,
and pink leatherette. They were cutely tacky. I asked if he'd take
care of export filings and delivery to a ship in port. He nodded
eagerly. When I mentioned tomorrow, he laughed. He thought I
was joking. I shrugged, letting it pass for the time being. He had
a huge supply of rush tiles but only a small supply of tulip nuts,
which he said got rancid if stored too long. I put them on my list.
I mentioned the Madras, fingering the bolts he fanned in front
of me. He was beginning to believe in a sale. He shouted for tea,
which was brought out by a wan, pop-eyed counterboy.

Over tea we relaxed, chatting war and love as blandly as the
weather. The exporter leaned against his doorjamb in a ray of sunlight. With two heavy fingers he dug crumpled black mint leaves
from his glass and flung them to the dirt outside. Almost friendly
now, he called the counterboy back and ordered him to show me a
special item. It was a pigskin dildo, very cunningly sewn, with some
of the bristle left intact toward the base to suggest pubic hair.

I was holding this object and listening to the renewed rumble
of shells outside the city when I realized what I was doing was
insane. There wasn't any time. I was deceiving myself, not Dadi
Anton. I may have blushed. I know the temperature of my skin
changed instantly. Making a slight but real effort to convince the
exporter I'd come back, I set aside the dildo and clapped my hands

to signal wrapping up. I felt a frisson of irrational panic that the man wouldn't let me out unless I bought his crap. I hid the fear well enough. He frowned stolidly in the doorway. I had to turn sideways to slide past him.

I WAS TOO AFRAID to go back to the hotel—or I didn't want to know what was happening there. I lay in wait drinking coffee in a ship's chandler's doorway, until I saw the *Narses* return. The faces aboard and on the dock were grim. They were worried about the situation in the city, or the ship hadn't handled well. I had an intuition talking to the ship's officers about my cargo wouldn't go over well just then. I waited for Van Loon to appear. Deep in conversation with two men, he came from behind one of the huge piles of deal on deck. All three men kept fingering the half-inch rope of the cargo netting that held the piles in place. The discussion went on for a long time, until two dockworkers threw down a wooden ramp with a herringbone of black sandpaper glued to it, that served as gangplank. Van Loon ended his conversation with a shrug. The moment he set foot on the gangplank I called to him. He came off the ship but seemed to have trouble focusing his thoughts. I handed him the last of my coffee. He took a sip and made a face.

"Sweet!" Finally he looked at me, registering the fact I liked sweet coffee—and my presence—with a smile of pleasure. "I'm glad you got the note. Really glad," he said. "I've been busy."

Even though I was anxious for myself and for the treasure, I felt a wave of concern for Van Loon and led him to sit with me on one of the huge davits the idiot had cleaned. I was at my most controlled, my most calming. I told myself I was getting ready to make the delicate argument for putting my boxes aboard. But maybe there was also real affection. He rubbed his red-rimmed eyes and raised his face to the sky, which was blue but, to the east, dirty—a stain scrubbed into a film—smoke from the shelling in that direction had diffused completely.

My gaze rested on Van Loon. Exhausted myself, I sank to a low level of existence the moment I sat down. I seemed to see past what he looked like—wax bust of a boy that's taken a turn over a flame—and stared too deeply, out-of-true. The stubble on a cheek just beginning to melt into a jowl, reddish curls lank in the heat, produced an effect on me like erotic stupidity, except desire was absent. Maybe an infant feels that kind of stunned bodily fascination for a parent's hand or cheek or neck. It was a kind of closeness, anyway.

A bomb startled me. "Carter," I began. "There's one thing. I've taken care of passage but I have some cargo and I can't go without it."

"That's what we were just talking about," he said dully. "They think half-inch gauge is only good enough for hatch netting. And if there's too much pitch, they're worried some of the boards could slip forward through the net."

"The holds are full?"

"Full up, yeah." He looked at me. "What do you mean you have cargo? You got something while you were here?"

"I've had it all along."

"You had it in B? How'd you get it out?"

"On the *Myrrha*."

"Can I ask what it is?"

There wasn't any point in secrecy now. It felt awkward to tell him though, since I'd avoided telling him before. Worse, I thought I heard the beginnings of suspicion in his voice. "Well, it's coin," I said. "Not a lot. I have twenty-four boxes, small boxes, pretty heavy though. Together they weigh something shy of a ton."

He couldn't help folding his arms. In an effort not to seem startled, he nodded his head thoughtfully.

I decided I had to be up-front. "It's not the gold. Or any part of it. Why do people think that? It's silver I've had all along, silver that belongs to my shippers. I'll show you. I already have to show Anders Willis. In fact, I have to go back for the inspection right away. I should be there now. I don't know why . . ."

"So they interviewed you," he stalled.

"You know I'm telling the truth. You tried to find out about the gold yourself. You told me that insurrectionist group, whatever it was, found the treasure and . . ."

"Right. No, we've figured that—well, basically, that the shells they've been throwing at us—" He gestured at the faint copper of the eastern sky. "That's where the gold went. Most of it anyway."

"I didn't feel like telling you before, because—I was too secretive. Or afraid. It looks ridiculous now. I realize that. You must think—"

"What I think isn't the issue, is it?" He was perceptibly less friendly. "The problem is I arranged space aboard for you, not for more cargo. They aren't going to like it. I don't even know if there'll be time to load tomorrow morning."

"I know there's room. I didn't tell you—I *also* didn't tell you—but I found out about the *Narses* on my own, and I booked passage before I got your note. So that means there's double the room, right?"

This second surprise confused him even more, and his expression of doubt deepened. "I think space is only one problem. The other is weight and loading."

"You could tell them it was part of the Mandarins' cargo."

"I could. I guess I could insist."

"Please."

"About the space issue—really there're only one or two spots I can think of. But we'd have to measure them. I don't know how big your boxes are. And you'd have to bring them down today. Soon."

As soon as I'd mentioned it out loud, I couldn't stop thinking about getting back to the Colebart for the Anders Willis inspection. I closed my eyes in angry frustration. I'd wasted so much time pawing though Madras and loitering over coffee!

When I opened my eyes, Van Loon was staring at me as if he thought my expression meant I was angry at him. "You know you could have told me. You should have," he said.

"I know. I know."

"I was never out to get you."

"No," I echoed, chidden.

"You can't always play things so close to the vest."

"For me, it's normal."

That must have come out sounding a little cross, because he

stood, eyebrows raised, muttering in the direction of the *Narses*. "Look, if you don't get it—if you don't get how to behave with people, I can't teach you."

It occurred to me to complain about the omissions on his side, but I didn't say anything. I felt too pressed for time. With a big show of neutrality, Van Loon led me on to the ship. Heading forward, we circled one of the huge piles of lumber. The area around the windlass, the utmost foredeck of the *Narses*, was canopied in steel. On top of the canopy deal was stacked several feet deep in a complicated chevron pattern. Underneath, where the great root of the bowsprit angled in, head, forepeak hatch, and windlass were clustered. A tiny pen for a hog or two was built along the starboard curvature of the bow. On the other side a goat was chained. Kneeling on straw, it eyed us with devilish poise.

Van Loon gestured, saying that he'd thought, perhaps, here . . .

Swallowing impatience, I said, "No. No, it can't be out on deck." Nodding as if he'd known it wouldn't be good enough for me, Van Loon led me aft and below deck, explaining there was a tiny hold with secret access from the captain's saloon. The space was ordinarily reserved for the captain's personal use. With everything topsy-turvy, the captain in the first mate's cabin, he and I in the saloon, he'd been planning on using the space for his own baggage.

The glass in the saloon windows cast a wormy light. Van Loon pulled a small horsehair divan to the middle of the room. He knelt and twisted two wooden dowels, which had worn yellow circles in the finish of a mahogany dado. He lifted the panel away. I knelt beside him to peer into the hold and let myself slump against his shoulder briefly in relief. "Perfect."

"Better than forward with the goat," he said. "But still, they're not going to like more weight so high up, right under the deck."

"It's not that much," I reassured him silkily. "You and I could handle the boxes. Or I'll hire somebody."

When we left the saloon, a reedy shadow grabbed my forearm, and the ex-waiter's laughing voice piped, "Lucky dog! You get to stay back here with the fancy crowd. I'm stuck forward, and you wouldn't believe! You have to promise you'll protect me, please. I'm serious. Or let me come back sometimes, if that's allowed."

I nodded and rubbed his shoulder hurriedly, careful of the bruises. It was awkward, but I wasn't going to brush him off just because Van Loon was with me. Glancing back, I caught an odd frown of dignity on Van Loon's face as he asked us in surprise, "You two know each other?"

WHEN I RAN into the Colebart, the day clerk, wearing an expression of terror and exasperation, gave me a huge open-armed shrug—"Finally!"—which would have been comical, but two unfriendly boys were standing next to him holding guns, claret berets pulled low over their brows. Looking up the elevator shaft in explanation, all the clerk got out was, "Sir—!" I glowered briskly at the soldiers and ran up the spiral stair.

On the sixth floor I saw a man in foulard boxers, another guest, withdrawing timidly behind his door. My room was open. A pass-key hung from the door-lock. I went into the shower room. The metal door was open. Rope hung from the inner handle, untied, not cut. Through the open closet I could see the Masonite panel on the other side had split when they pried it open. Two soldiers, an officer and three other men were in the shower room. Two of the civilians, in short-sleeved suits, I guessed were government. The third, wearing a blue oxford and khakis, looked like Anders Willis. The officer, who wasn't ECOMILG but a national army major, was poking around the far reaches of the room. The civilians talked. The inspection was almost over. The cardboard carton of buttons had been dragged from the closet. The blue boxes had all been taken from the shelves and lined up on the floor.

I'd never been in the shower room at this hour, and for the first time I saw that, when the sun was full on the front of the hotel, it shone through innumerable scratches in the painted "Colebart" sign covering the windows. It looked almost like an incandescent script, but instead of lighting the room, the letters created a golden haze that made it even more difficult to see. In that light the inspectors might even have thought my silver was gold. The major strode out of the haze. I decided he was the one I had to deal with. But not at first.

As confidently as I could, I walked straight to the three civilians, apologizing offhandedly for being late. "I'm sure you're all incredibly pressed right at the moment." That was no guess. Shelling had been increasing hour by hour. The nervous atmosphere all over the city felt particularly dangerous in the shower room. But I wanted to appear composed. The only safety would be in acting as if this were the most normal thing in the world, acting that way so compellingly that everyone else went along. "Let's get it over with, if we can. Do you need me to show you, or have you already taken a look?"

"We've looked. We couldn't wait," said one of the government people. He waggled a standard duty form, on which he'd scrawled something carelessly.

The Anders Willis man looked with some alarm at the two young soldiers, who were just bending over to lift one of the blue boxes. The other government man raised his eyebrows at the major, a silent remark that wasn't too broad for the farthest balcony in an opera house. I didn't know what was going on, what they'd been discussing, but I could think of one possibility. I started talking and hoped no explosions would interrupt the soothing rhythm of my voice.

I talked about my shippers, how convenient it had been that two of them had a friend at Anders Willis—though not surprising, since they did business all over the world—and yet were fond of me, trusted me (as anyone could see by the treasure), which was not an everyday quality among extremely powerful businessmen—at least not in Z—but the big city was an unforgiving place, wasn't it? I was careful not to overdo it—this wasn't opera, after all—but somewhere in the middle of my spiel I stopped myself and turned to the two soldiers, who'd finally lifted that box, "You know, there's no need—I don't know if you feel like you have to put everything back exactly the way it was—but there's no need. I can handle the boxes myself. I have a bunch of guys I've hired." I turned back to the others. "In any case, I was surprised myself to have lucked into a connection with men like that . . ."

Finally, the major spoke. "We're happy you got safely back to the hotel, sir. Among other things, we were just talking about warning you that the city isn't going to be at all safe tonight. It's

probably a good night to stay inside, no?" The two soldiers lowered the box they were holding and let go of the rope handles.

"That's very good advice, sir." I tipped open the loose-jointed
flaps of the old carton of buttons. "Did you find these, as well?"
I asked. Everyone was nodding. Even so I peered in and saw the
two additional blue boxes, including the one with a scratched lid.
"I see you did. Good." I looked at the major solemnly. "These two
might be easiest to carry. The one isn't full. I'm sure you noticed.
You could stack it on top of the other, and two strong guys could
carry them between them." I glanced at the soldiers.

The major allowed himself a creeping grin. "You seem to think
we don't take our work seriously."

"Just the opposite," I said. "I can tell how serious you are. This
is a serious affair. It's a lot of money. I'm one man, and I have no
protection at all."

He seemed to like that. He nodded agreeably and said, "Exactly
why I warn you, it would be a terrible thing for you to leave the
hotel." He nodded to the soldiers, who came and lifted the boxes
noisily from the drift of brass buttons. The civilians looked around
in embarrassment. When they all left the shower room, the major
himself carried his own and his soldiers' guns in an awkward sheaf.

I figured if the major didn't send the two boys at the desk for
another load right away, I had at best two hours before he changed
his mind. I bolted the shower room from the inside and crawled
through the broken Masonite into my room. In the hall, I locked
the door and kept the passkey as well as my room key.

11

I NEEDED TO CALL Topher. The doodled-on notebook was right
where I'd left it this morning. The phone must have been in use all
day. Several other hands had scrawled numbers in the margins of
my windowless city, as well as an underlined notation, "At Nine
No Bags Gen. Wils. Ave. off Suff."

I had to call Topher. My first attempt I got a westernizing
recorded message: "Due to an emergency situation and heavy calling volume . . ." Phone service wasn't going to last much longer.
The next time I got a ring, but it was cut off by a busy signal. At
least that gave me hope. The fifth time I dialed, Topher answered
on the fourth ring. He hung up on me. I stared at the receiver,
feeling wronged and frantic. I had to dial six more times to get

through. Apparently he was lying on the cot with the phone, because he picked up before the first ring finished.

"I'm calling to say goodbye," I said quickly. I heard him breathing. I couldn't not imagine the smell of it, the warmth. "Why the hell did you hang up on me?" I snapped. That got no response, either. "Please, Tophe, *Tophe*, you've got to get out of the city. It can't be safe where you are. I was going to ask you to help me with the boxes again. But that's beside the point. There's an extra place reserved on the *Narses*. It hasn't been paid for, but I'll pay it, even if you don't help me with the boxes."

I waited. I heard an indefinite vowel or just a small moan. Then Topher cut it short and said, "Goodbye." He hung up.

I'd told him, "That's beside the point," but now, frowning and too tense to know what I felt, getting my boxes out of the city seemed to be the only point. My low purposefulness, like a shark's, came with a mere ghost of an emotion, which, I swear, despite everything, was pleasurable—happiness of a dark sort. Outside, I saw the streets were deserted. It was going to be all but impossible to find a strong man or two to hire. I could only hope the major hadn't left someone behind to watch the hotel.

The waterfront was empty. Sufferance Street was empty. I started heading east in despair, but that neighborhood was empty, too, as usual. The sun was setting. As I searched street after street, I kept coming face to face with it. The roadway would fill with dancing black discs, then slowly empty. The longer this took, the more my thoughts focused on the flimsy locks keeping hôtelier, showering guests, soldiers, and the world from my treasure.

I wasn't at all sure it was good luck when I spotted a muleteer crouching to shit in a condemned doorway. His mule and rough, two-wheeled cart were drawn up on the sidewalk. I watched. The man took a long time. But he looked insane, not constipated. He'd lifted his vacant, almost cheerful, face skyward and turned it side to side as if he were following a tennis ball. It didn't look right. Near where he'd stopped a pile of black filth clogged the gutter. That wasn't unusual in Alejandrina, but anyone normal would have chosen another spot. Worse, it looked like the man was being stalked by two starving dogs. Heads low, the animals jogged around him in a semicircle, split up, retraced their path. The mule jerked its tackle with fretful nods and whimpered, then screamed.

The dogs lunged—this sudden action came like a blow to my solar plexus—attacking not the muleteer but the pile of filth. An enormous cloud of flies rose with a terrifying hum audible from across the street. Underneath was a slack, pale blue body in a sarong, its foot gnawed off. Rising into an unseen ray of sunlight, the flies glittered, a whirling cloud of gold dust. Below, the dogs were only able to drag the body a foot or so. They snapped furiously at the flies when they started to resettle.

I dug all the silver dollars I had from my pockets and spread them on the upturned palms of my hands. Like a supplicant, I crossed the street, approaching the lunatic muleteer to ask for help even before he wiped himself or stood up. The dogs shied and glared at me balefully.

· · ·

I HAD TO PAY another guest, the man in the foulard boxers, ten dollars to help me get the boxes downstairs and into the mule cart. When I settled my bill, I gave the day clerk such a large tip that he helped with a box or two as he was going off duty. I tipped the night clerk to keep him silent. With only twenty-two boxes the job went a little faster. Though I was as good as renegade at this point, I couldn't help, like a proper supercargo, running through the figures—Muleteer $16; Colebart $237; Tip $5; Hired man $10; Day Clerk Tip $12; Night Clerk Tip $10; Travel Expenses $22. Only 1,188 silver dollars remained in the twenty-second box, on the lid of which I scratched a cross. $2,188 had gone to the major. $812 for passage and earlier expenses. I was left $32,688 of the original $36,000.

I dusted my shins and felt the bruises underneath. As the muleteer and I were leaving, Topher showed up in a sweat. He'd obviously run most of the way from the eastern quarter. The boy didn't apologize or smile or touch me. He met my gaze, but only briefly. Despite the long run, now that he'd found me he acted sullen. He fell into step beside me as I walked behind the cart. With boxes piled on the seats and the muleteer perched on top there was no room inside. "I'm glad you decided to come, Topher. There's nothing for you here. Not for a long time, anyway." I was perfectly sincere. I calculated his passage might cost me $1,000, since we were so late.

"I'm not coming. I'm saying goodbye, I think."

His uncertainty made me reflect. The less he said the more power he had over me, and I wondered if he didn't know that, if it wasn't the reason he was being so closemouthed. He kept looking up and down streets, around corners. Caution was natural on a night like that, but he looked like he was searching for a particular route, not on the alert for danger. He had to know I was headed to the port. We were going a roundabout way, because I wanted to avoid the main streets as well as the narrowest alleys.

When we came to a crossroads where we'd have to turn irrevocably to the waterfront, Topher brushed my arm and said, "I want to ask you something." I waited. "Remember, I've never asked you for anything. I want to ask if you'll please come with me somewhere for an hour. Then you can go down to the ship."

"How can I do that?" I looked at the cart full of treasure. "Maybe after I load——"

"No. It has to be now."

I couldn't read his face. He seemed serious, but how did I know it wasn't another irrelevant trip to show me what a tidy housekeeper he was? He was a kid, after all. Even tonight, different things might be important to him. "I can't. I have to stay with the boxes."

"This guy can come with us. The whole cart."

"It's too dangerous."

"It's not. Where we're going is safe. It's not even in the city, but not far. I promise." His T-shirt was as thin as tissue paper, and it hadn't dried yet. Little breezes, forerunners of the storm, which was late today, toyed with the shirt. The cloth kept sticking to his body and letting go with kissing hesitation. Or a gust would press the cloth revealingly against some part of his torso.

"So you'll come with me? I can't believe this! I'm asking you nothing." His feet stayed on the ground, but his body hopped slightly in frustration.

"Sh. Sh, I know, Topher. I have to take care of the boxes."

The muleteer chuckled. He'd turned around and watched us contentedly from atop the load.

"We'll take them with us I said,"Topher pleaded.

"What is it you want?"

"Please come."

"I don't have time." I shook my head in the direction of the sea. The muleteer started laughing, and I couldn't help shouting at him, "What are you laughing about?"

"Hard on your friend," he croaked.

"Please come," Topher repeated.

"Where are we going?"

"Please come."

"Around and around," the muleteer murmured.

"I'll come, if you promise to leave with me on the *Narses*."

"Fine," he said in a tone that made it plain he could get out of that promise later.

Topher and I walked ahead, mule and cart following closely. The mule was large and could have been taken for a horse except for its big donkey ears which perked and flickered. The animal wasn't happy in caravan. Whenever I looked back, it half turned its head to fix me with a huge, alarmed eye. Then it lowered its head, not dull obedience but conniving. So I imagined. The trip was like a poor echo of *Varanath Prin*. More so as we went on.

It took us about fifteen minutes to reach the scrub at the northern outskirts of town. From there it wasn't far over a human cow path into real jungle. Fat, scattered drops of rain had been falling for some time. Yet all of us were hot, in a sweat. Each time a

raindrop hit a sensitive spot we shivered, then immediately felt
the heat and the sweat more keenly. After passing into the jungle
the rain made a widespread tapping, and we were spared getting
soaked.

We trudged silently. I'd decided this was a foolish detour, as
bad as my trip to the exporter's. But the bitter thought simply
floated there. I'd sunk to the lowest imaginable level of existence.
My eyes kept dropping to Topher's haunches, his butt, its slovenly
side-to-side so beautiful to me. The silence felt heavenly. I was
calm. Topher's beauty must have sweetened the general dread.
Not just sweetened but intensified it, brought out its actual fla-
vor—anything but the distraction beauty is thought to be.

Exactly like the last time I was in the jungle, we came to a
clearing, which must have been a Karak village once. Near the
center was one of those ominous corrugated steel buildings. In
the rain, it sounded as if its bolts were bursting. We shifted two
muddy motorbikes and maneuvered the cart and mule under a
shed attached to the building, which had a murky sheet of plastic
in place of a door. Topher stood in front of the plastic, folded his
arms and bowed his head. He waved a crane fly from his torn ear.
"You're going to be really angry . . ." he said.

My heart sank. "Nice ambush," I whispered.

"It's not like that. I made a promise to Bill Sawtell—"

"Shit."

"He's my friend. I had to. He needs to talk to you. I told him
you were going on the *Narses*. He made me promise—if I could
bring you before you left. Remember his brother died up there.
It's as simple as that. You're the only one who saw him."

"What do you owe this Sawtell person?"

"Nothing. I do it as a friend. I made a promise. Plus—" He lowered his voice and looked behind him. "—I told you before, the guy is sort of in love with me."

"So because he loves you, you owe him? How does that work? All I do is love somebody, and they have to do whatever I say? That's crazy. You don't owe the guy anything just because he's got some random fixation on you."

"You would say that."

"Of course, I would. You're not somebody's toy. People can't pick you up and say, 'Oh, I'm into this guy, so it's *justice* that he has to be into me, no matter what kind of pig or monster I am.'"

"Big talker," Topher said scornfully. "You always twist things your way, don't you?"

"You're not listening to me. You're a kid. Why can't we just say goodbye like friends? What does anything that happened in B have to do with you and me?"

"I thought you said you wanted me to come with you. *Not* say goodbye."

"I said you had to get out. You do. There *is* a spot on the *Narses*, and I *will* pay for it. You're crazy if you pass up the opportunity. Hell, I should *make* you go. Anyone who really cared about you would say, 'Go! Go!'"

"But you don't necessarily want me to come?"

"Oh, shit. Topher—" I covered my face with my hands.

"You probably feel guilty."

"I do." I sighed.

"Then just talk to him."

"No, Topher. No. I don't feel guilty about Sawtell or about what happened in B. I feel guilty . . . " I had no idea why I felt guilty. It made no sense. Even at the time, the grandiose notion that my desire was too harsh for Topher seemed like bullshit—that there was something noble about holding back. I felt it, but I didn't buy it. I envied the captain's love for the boy as a wholehearted thing, unlike mine, but I thought it was probably ignorant, too. Maybe Topher wanted me to tell him, "Come live with me forever in Z." It would have sounded worse than a lie, worse than a fantasy. Saying goodbye, on the other hand, was tragic. "Probably I should feel guilty about what happened in B. Instead of about you." I couldn't believe I was letting the boy get away with his silly argument from emotion. I was tired.

"Guilty about me? I'm fine."

Maybe that was it. I couldn't imagine him fine. For me, he was an all-vulnerable notion from the lowest level of existence, one that couldn't possibly survive in the open air.

"Just talk to him," Topher repeated.

"What can I say to him? Why do you need to harass me about B?"

"I'm not harassing you. But it's different. You're different. It doesn't affect you the same way as me—I mean, as Bill."

"How do you see that?"

"And anyway, if it was something like you loved me, and what I did—tricking you into coming up here—if that turned out to really hurt you, well, that would be different."

"I'm not hurt?"

"No. I don't know if you can be. But screw it. This was all about Bill. I did it as a friend." He wasn't going to cry. It was the nightingale glub-glub that got into his voice when he used words like "friend." He let his anger work itself up. "This is about Bill. His brother died up there! That's the kind of love we should be talking about! And since you just breezed out of B on the *Myrrha*, the least you can do now is tell him what happened—especially since maybe you made a little profit off the whole deal."

"What? I haven't made anything in this fucking country."

"I meant the gold."

I laughed. "Right. I forgot you weren't there for the inspection. So you think I have the gold? Why is everybody so sure I have gold I don't have? Why don't you take a look in my boxes right now?"

"No. I don't care. Maybe you don't have it."

"I don't." I walked over to the mule and rested my head against its flank for a moment. Its heart was racing. The rain was coming on harder now. A glossy fringe of water scalloped the edge of the shed's roof. I touched it. The mule nudged my elbow. I looked into its huge eye. When it snorted gently, a thread of mucus snapped on to its muzzle. The tongue came lumbering out and patted around its lips.

"Let me get him," Topher said quietly. He sounded resigned, even depressed. He pushed open the plastic sheet with a hint of frustrated roughness. Inside, the building was dim. I could make out what looked like cages along both sides. A naked, emaciated man may have been hunched in the corner of one. I wasn't sure. In front of each row of cages, a small channel had been cut in the dirt on either side of a wide, packed-earth corridor running down the middle. The two channels joined at the far end of the building and went out through a kind of scupper. A rusty brown and black residue in the channels looked like blood to me. Topher couldn't possibly know what was going on here, I thought. I didn't understand it myself. I assumed Anders Willis was closing up shop in the country and had set Sawtell adrift. This had to be his new job, whatever it was.

I had no chance to think more about the building, which was just as well, because those thoughts were so confused and dark. Sawtell appeared. I don't remember seeing his eyes, which means he never looked at mine, which means he came at me in a brute, unthinking rage. I must have pushed his head down to my chest. I remember the feel of a boulder in my arms, phenomenal energy behind it. I was on the mud, out in the rain. Turning to land face forward, I'd hit my forehead on the cement block base of one of the pipes holding up the shed.

I twisted back and grabbed Sawtell's head again. Though it was slick with his hair, I had enough of a grip to try shoving it against the cement block. His neck resisted. I wasn't in the frame of mind to fight. He had more strength. Still, I tried to give his head a second, harder shove. It didn't seem fair that Topher and two men from inside the building dragged Sawtell off me before I had the chance.

Topher helped me up. He used the apron of his shirt to wipe my forehead. "Nice ambush," I said again. "Nice ambush." I didn't believe it, but I was enraged.

"That was not supposed to happen. That was not supposed to happen," he kept repeating.

I had my hands on his shoulders. No matter how angry I was, I could feel the softness and the shifting of his muscles. Pretending to need him for balance, I pulled him forward a bit, until our faces and chests just felt the warmth of the other's body. Then, like pendula, we swung apart slightly. After lifting my palms from his shoulders, I never touched him again.

OF ALL THE PEOPLE aboard the *Narses*, I was the sole passenger. Everyone else had a job. Since my lack of an occupation was unique, maybe it had a nuance of the exemplary, the useful even. Even during that first busy night when the shouting never stopped—nor the sound of bare feet shuffling across the deck nor the squeal of ropes wound on thick pegs nor the dreadful collapsing noise of chains laid aside. It was decided Alejandrina might not last the night, so we left early, at midnight. I don't know of anyone we left behind.

A sort of calm, or a general stupor, prevailed by the next evening. After dinner's two seatings in the narrow, neck-high galley, the ex-waiter curled up on the bench next to me, hiding from more work. A black enamel pot of coffee rocketed dolorously (without ever rising) on a blue flame on the range. The timbers creaked with tiny heartbeat steps as the ship swayed. The greasy varnish of the bulkheads reflected pairs of gleams, blue and yellow, gas flame and oil lamp.

Drifting to attention, I looked down and found the ex-waiter's eyes on me and tried to imagine what he could be thinking. Maybe he nursed a hope that my stroking his head repetitively like a kitten . . . that the pleasantness of it could accumulate into permanence. Or maybe he wanted the stroking to wipe away his last confused awe for any fabulous notions of eternity.

He pulled my fingers into his mouth, and I ran them slowly along the rippled surface of his molars. The cook poured coffee for two sailors who sat and drank in haste across the table. The spider's silk that held me outside the scene broke. I was really there, stuck and alone, stalling for no particular reason before I went and faced Van Loon. My experiences weren't being gone through for some future, ideal friend. I was really there.

IN THE JUNGLE near Alejandrina they were shining a flashlight in Sawtell's face. The shadows warpainted him but made it difficult to read his expression, which was what they needed. They were looking for the truth, and they knew Sawtell hated the gloomy supercargo (by which they meant me) enough to peddle any lie that could cause him trouble. If Sawtell had picked up the story from the blond kid he was fucking—or who was fucking him— or who was playing along until he had to drop his pants for a blow job, more likely—if he'd just picked up the story, they wouldn't have bothered. But the two others working here had seen a cart stacked with blue boxes the right size. The blond had gone already. The supercargo had left even earlier with the boxes.

Thick lashes going instantly long then short on the pale hoods of his eyes, Sawtell swore up and down that the kid had once let slip in a fit of anger this incontestable fact: the supercargo had spirited part of the missing gold out of B. The blond boy had loaded it on to the *Myrrha* with his own hands. He'd heard the coins chuckle with his own ears.

Flashlit briefly, the two other men shook their heads. They'd removed their rubber gloves in the damp heat, and one of them slapped his pair on the seat of his motorbike for emphasis. They'd seen the blue boxes, yes, but they hadn't heard them.

"What's the harm?" Sawtell said scornfully. His tone didn't go with the theatrical, lit-from-below expression of terror. "Everyone knows it's a fucking Mandarin cargo on the *Narses*. You take it, there's no gold, big deal. You'll have whatever else there is. The Mandarins are in bed with the insurrection. That's a well-known fact. Tomorrow, you'll see, I swear, they won't have touched anything Mandarin, but everything else—they're going to bomb the shit out of everything else."

AT THAT MOMENT the captain of the *Myrrha* sat bolt upright in his extra-wide bed. It wasn't a kind of movement he'd made before. No one who'd seen him would ever dream he could shift so much weight so rapidly. But he did. He was in pain. With normal slowness now, he scooted to the edge of the bed and eased himself to his feet. His underarms were intensely sore.

He knew Topher wasn't on the boat. Even so, full of terrible anxiety, the captain made his way—slowly, slowly—to the spot where he'd last seen the boy, which was in the pilothouse. He had his own strange purpose. Waves passed across his vision like the overlapping alertnesses of cocaine. Each instant of attention overtook the last in meaningless and distracting surges of lucidity. The captain was deeply frightened. To him, this felt like the turbulence

of time at the very end of life, not like the physical effects of car-
diovascular disease, or something more critical, which was likely
given the pain.

In the pilothouse he went to the stool Topher had been sitting
on. The captain understood he was alone—he hated it—but still
he wanted the company of, if not another person, then the trace
of another person, of someone he loved. And if the best he could
do was inhale where the loved one may have left some molecules
of himself, then the captain would do that. Unfortunately he
couldn't bend over, and the stool was too low. Dizzy, forcing his
body to bend, breathing in as deeply as he could, hunting for the
scent, the captain suddenly thought the stool was rising. Perhaps
it hit him on the cheek. He must have fallen. He got a hand to
the edge of the stool and was just able to raise his head. Instead
of Topher's musk, the last thing he noticed was his own hand, the
gleam of a gold ring and, from the ring next to it, the fascinating
glitter of the grille of diamonds.

WHEN I WOKE the *Narses* was in turmoil. We'd been dogged all
morning by a pirate. Van Loon, who'd been on deck, told me the
enemy had popped in and out of sight for hours while fog thickened. Now the fog was too dense to see farther than a hundred
feet or so. The other worry was the ignorant crew, most of them
fresh from the crimps' hands and worse than useless. When I went
on deck to look for myself, I found the ship surrounded by half-
silvered infinity. Somehow the sun was getting in. Looking into the
fog felt like fainting.

In controlled panic the officers were lining up the newest sailors with clubs. The chumps were wearing whatever they'd had on when grabbed. They shivered. Their thin shirts were puke-stained or muddy. Again and again, the officers clubbed hands to sides, feet and shins till the men stood in a straight line. They struck faces they decided were clenched in defiance or too relaxed in dumb terror. Blood flecked the deck. They shouted the lessons. It was pointless in the end. No one had any time to learn. Someone shouted when he saw a shadow in the cloud.

Since the fog made for a close white backdrop, what happened—a sort of battle—seemed mad and isolated like those islets of punishment in imaginary hells. For a surprisingly long time it was hard to tell whether the shadow was coming at us or passing by. Some of the sailors, even the new ones, were issued carbines from ship's meager armory. Men crouched among the mazes of deal, though the piles were so tall they didn't need to.

The moment the other ship came into focus, the enemy played bold and started firing. We answered. The whole thing was nonsensical, because no one could see. The other ship seemed to shrink and move faster as it came out of the fog. It wasn't large. Someone said a barquentine, black tricked out in purple. It was coming on at an angle that looked too oblique to ram us effectively.

Everyone on both sides of the gap between ships was firing in total confusion. The few successful shots I saw had more to do with murder than war. One of the crimps' victims, who'd lost an incisor to a club a little earlier, had been given a carbine. He stationed himself about forty feet and somewhat behind the second mate who'd clubbed the tooth from his head. His first

bullet splintered the deck by the mate's heel. I started shouting.
But everyone was shouting. The second bullet hit the deck, too.
A splinter may have tickled the mate, because he reached back to
rub his ankle without ever turning to see his own sailor firing on
him, improving his aim. When the mate started taking bullets, he
rubbed and scratched himself harder, first calf then hip as they
were hit in turn.

I was sure the killer wouldn't fire on me, so I ran to the second mate. Crouching next to him so my body blocked him from
behind, I told him he'd been shot—three times at that point. The
fact I had to tell him shows how useless our .22 or .25 caliber
ammunition was. Still, everyone fired madly.

After I spoke, the second mate stared at me. He was a young
man with an old man's beard, a red bib that reached halfway down
his chest but was so sparse I could see his buttons through it. His
narrow, licked-looking eyebrows frowned over too young eyes.
"You've been shot three times," I repeated. I helped him scuttle
forward out of the line of fire, both lines of fire.

The two ships collided with a bass howl. The barquentine hit
the *Narses* toward the stern on the starboard side. It must have
been going faster than I guessed, because as it squealed alongside, the *Narses'* bow was slowly forced against the other ship's
stern. From belowdecks a watery, woody clangor rose as the two
hulls were sucked against each other when the ocean sluiced away
between them. The barquentine, much lower as well as smaller,
seemed to pry the *Narses* up from below. We listed to port. The
second mate and I grabbed at the wire of the hog pen.

I could hear the jingle of the goat's chain over the rest of the noise. I saw its hooves lose their grip on the deck as straw fluttered through the port rail. Hind legs knelt, forelegs splayed. The bleating animal made swimming motions against the deck trying to climb to starboard as the ship kept rolling. I thought I heard hull gliding against hull with a colossal stuttering. But the sound might have been boards breaking free of the cargo netting. The second mate lost his grip and fell past me along the near-vertical deck. He hit the goat which went over the port rail. The animal must not have broken its neck, because it managed a little hoarse bleating as its legs thrashed twenty feet or so above the water. From there the *Narses* spun over quickly. My gut lagged sickeningly when I was flung in an arc into the water.

The waves seemed to beat me with hammers. Everywhere the water made a loud barking. My eyes stung so badly from seawater, I couldn't see. Blindly, I got my arms around some of the boards from Green's Yard. Taking my weight they sank to a foot or so below the surface. A bigger armful was more buoyant but harder to manage. I raised my head as far as I could and blinked my eyes at the sky until tears came. I went on blinking, until I was able to see again, then looked around me.

There were no men, there was no *Narses*, the barquentine had gone. As far as I could see in every direction—not very far, because the glowing fog was still as heavy as before—the water was covered with yellow boards as if someone sloppy had tried to lay a parquet on the sea. The vast floor moved with the swells. It hammered me and clucked. Its seams parted to show the water gleaming dull white in whatever sunlight made it through the fog. I shivered from the cold and because I imagined my legs were hanging over an infinite and dark abyss.

After just a few minutes, time became impossible to judge. Even after I survived a night, it took superhuman concentration for me to count accurately the number times the sun had set and risen—one each! The sun burned the fog away, and it burned my neck and the places where my hair had stiffened in serried parts. The burns and the cut on my forehead were agony with the constant lapping of saltwater. Once or twice I tried to shuffle together a raft from the boards, but by afternoon of the first day—it may have been—only my own armful of wood was left. The rest of the floor had drifted away. I lay my arms across the loose bundle this way and that and tried to ignore how my skin was constantly pinched as the boards shifted in the waves. The wood was riding progressively lower in the water.

I must have dozed several times, and eventually salt glued my lashes together. I felt too weak to let go of the boards, so I tried pulling my eyes open the way a groggy man would. I managed a one-eyed, starry sort of vision. My cheek fell to a damp bit of board that rose out of the water.

I thought I saw a galleon with my good eye. Maybe as I came out of another faint. I made no effort hail it—ot that I could have raised my arms or screamed. The instant I *thought* I saw the ship, I was overwhelmed with relief, positive I was saved. Clearly I was delirious. I may have started crying in gratitude. The galleon became wobbly and even more indistinct. My confidence they would find me was so complete I started imagining what the galleon was like, filling in what I could barely see. The energy of the fantasy kept me from dwelling on my body—which by then was just numb flotsam seamed with pain. I was probably too weak to make any expression with the muscles of my face. But I remember the intense pleasure, the hope.

The galleon, I thought, was gilded on one side by the sun in the west. Even with perfect vision, I was too far away to see the sailors. But I saw them. Broad-leafed trees appeared to be growing amidships. The sailors lounged under them. Their rough hands were busy, though, as they fashioned miniature gardens with bridges of coconut hull and fountains of untwisted hemp. Knowing I was saved, I lingered over the models and the wonderful expressions of concentration on the handsome faces of the men.

ACKNOWLEDGEMENTS

Many people read this book in manuscript and commented help-fully. I'm especially grateful for Patrick Ryan's enthusiasm, because it came first, when I was unsure what to make of the book myself. I also want to thank Don Weise, Bob Smith, Michael Carroll, Richard Canning, Vestal McIntyre, Lisa Howorth, Everett McCourt, Bruno Navasky, Scott Manning, Thomas Keith, Patrick Merla, and Paul Florez. Darrell Crawford deserves my infinite gratitude, if only that were possible.